MW01601504

Unbreakable
Rise of the Unshakeable Woman

By: Unbreakable University

Unbreakable Rise of the Unshakeable Woman

Publishing by: Woman of Many
Trades LLC
Bronx, New York
Copyright 2025

UNBREAKABLE WOMAN MANTRA

I MAY BEND, I MAY SWAY,

I MAY STRETCH, AND I MAY SHAKE.

THERE'S NO WAY I WILL NEVER BREAK.

I AM AN UNBREAKABLE WOMAN.

BRIDGETT WHITNEY

We Got Werk to Do!

BY: ELEANOR NICOLE BROWN
WHEN THE STRUCTURE IS GONE
CHAT HAS ENDED
CLASS HAS CLOSED

WE GOT WERK TO DO WHEN NO
ONE IS NO LONGER WATCHING,
TALKING, OR TEACHING.
WE GOT WERK TO DO!

WHEN THE TEST BEGINS,
AND YOU'RE TAKING GUT PUNCH
AFTER GUT PUNCH.
WE GOT WERK TO DO!

WHEN THE OLD SELF TELLS YOU
"LAY DOWN. YOU NEED YOUR
REST." WE GOT WERK TO DO!

"IT'S ONLY ONE TIME," STOP IT!
PUT THAT MESS DOWN. WE GOT
WERK TO DO!

WHEN FAMILY AND FRIENDS CONSTANTLY REMIND YOU OF THE OLD SELF. WE GOT WERK TO DO!

WHEN IT'S ONLY YOU ROOTING 4 YOU, KEEP GOING! WE GOT WERK TO DO

WHEN THE WALLS START CLOSING IN, GET THAT ASS UP! WE GOT WERK TO DO

Unbreakable We Stand

Unbreakable, we stand, unyielding and firm.
Letting go of the past to walk where we belong.
Bendable, yes, but never undone, shedding old skin,
this battle is won.

We are powerful, unique, and learning to discern
the lessons of life through each twist and turn.
Beautiful, sharp, and brilliantly wise, rising each time,
like a phoenix that flies. Fighting, kicking, screaming,
we break the cycles of trauma we refuse to take.

Generations may bind, but we cut the chain. No longer
will sorrow and hurt remain. Used and played, but
those days are gone. Unbreakable we stand, steadfast
and strong.

With boundaries firm and demands in hand, we clear
the way for resilience to take hold of this land.
Brokenness, begone, small minds, step aside. Our
purpose is clear, and in truth, we confide.

Resilience and grace form the roots of our plan.
Unbreakable we stand, together we rise.

By: Ebony Brinson

This is Who We Are

U – Unyielding:

I stand firm, unmoved, unbothered, and undefeated by the forces that once tried to devour me. My spirit cannot be shaken. My purpose cannot be stolen.

N – Never Giving Up:

I refuse to quit. Every setback fuels my comeback. Every challenge strengthens my calling.

B – Believing I Am Enough:

I am enough, not for the approval of others, not to meet anyone else's expectations, but because I was created enough. I choose me, for me.

R – Reminding Myself:

I can do anything I set my mind, heart, and faith to. No dream too distant. No vision is too bold. No purpose too big for the God within me.

E – Elevate and Expand:

I will not limit my dreams to what's comfortable. I will elevate my thinking, expand my horizons, and reach heights even my younger self never dared to imagine.

A – Accountability:

I own my growth. I take responsibility for my healing, my purpose, and my destiny. No excuses. Just evolution.

K – Keep the Faith:

When doubt creeps in, I hold on to the unshakable truth: "I can do all things through Christ who strengthens me." My faith is my foundation.

A – Awaken:

Awakening to the power within me, tapping into the greatness God planted in my soul, ready to live, love, and lead with divine purpose.

B – Boldness:

I move boldly, unafraid, unashamed, walking fully in the power of who I am called to be.

L – Love:

Leading with love, love for God, love for others, love for myself because love is my power, my weapon, and my legacy.

E – Evolving:

Evolving every single day into the woman I was born to become, the woman God destined, anointed, and prepared me to be. Becoming HER, fully, fearlessly, and faithfully. This is my story. This is my strength. I. Am. UNBREAKABLE!

By: Shannon D. Perkins

Table of Contents

Dr. Tameika A. Marrow

Introduction: Forging Unbreakable Women

Life has a funny way of showing up with exactly what you need, usually when you least expect it, and often when you're not even sure you're ready. For me, that moment came not in a pulpit, a therapist's office, or a conference room. It came during something as simple as scrolling on TikTok. It wasn't unusual. Like most of us, I had moments where I would grab my phone and get lost in the rabbit hole of endless content. But this particular day was different. This time, it wasn't just entertainment. It was alignment. I stumbled across a man named Joseph Gause, and the moment I heard him speak, it was as if the atmosphere shifted. He wasn't talking to just anyone; he was talking to me. Every word felt like a mirror reflecting the strength I hadn't fully claimed. His message was simple, but it hit me like thunder: "Your past does not have to dictate your future. Strength is built from within."

Something inside of me awakened. I followed Joseph's live sessions not out of curiosity but out of necessity. He was teaching a new way to see yourself, a raw, unfiltered accountability that exposed your excuses and demanded your healing. When Joseph spoke about a course that would walk people through their purpose journey, I didn't hesitate. I was standing at a crossroads in my life, and I was finally ready to pivot. I didn't know it at the time, but I was about to walk into one of the most powerful transformations of my life. The course didn't just change me; it called me. I began to live in a way that felt whole, alive, and in alignment.

I was finally breathing in purpose with every step. Then came the call that shifted my role from student to steward. After seeking the Creator's direction, Joseph called me and said, "I want you to direct this next course. It's time." I remember the silence on the other end as I held the phone, feeling the weight of that moment press against my chest. I was honored, yes, but also overwhelmed. This wasn't just a job; this was a mantle, this was a responsibility, this was a divine assignment. He was entrusting me with the very thing that had saved me, and now I was being asked to become the vessel through which others would find the same freedom. So, Unbreakable Woman was born not as a cute title but as a movement, as a standard, and as a call to rise.

I didn't step into this lightly. I knew that if I was going to lead, I had to lead with integrity. This meant establishing structure, discipline, and accountability from the very beginning. No fluff and no sugar-coating. We were building warriors, not wanderers. I made it clear to every woman enrolling in this program: This is not for the faint of heart. You will be tested, you will be stretched, and if you're not willing to show up for yourself consistently, truthfully, and courageously, you will not last.

We started with nearly fifty women. They came in hungry, hurt, and hopeful. They came carrying years of trauma, generational pain, silent shame, and untapped potential. Many were used to being overlooked or undervalued, but they came. That alone was the first act of bravery. For six weeks, we journeyed together five nights a week. We meditated, we journaled, we exercised, we cried, we confessed, and we confronted truths we had buried for decades. There were no shortcuts. Every day requires discipline. Every night required vulnerability. Through that process, something sacred began to happen. I watched women peel back layers of pain. I watched them wrestle with identity. I watched them break open, and then I watched them rise. We created an environment that not only fostered growth but also demanded transformation.

The course itself wasn't just hard; it was holy. It became a sanctuary where brokenness was met with truth, where fear was silenced by action, and where women who had once seen themselves as victims began to roar with the sound of victory. What we experienced over those six weeks cannot be reduced to a syllabus. This was not a classroom. This was a crucible. Every class, every conversation, every tear, every breakthrough was forging something unshakeable, not just in them but in me.

Unbreakable Woman became more than a course; it became a mirror, a fire, a sisterhood, a movement, and now, you hold in your hands the fruit of that journey. This book is not fiction. It's not a theory. It's truth wrapped in testimony. These are real women who did the work, faced the fire, and chose to become Unbreakable. This is their story. Our story. Perhaps it's about to become your story, too.

As you turn these pages, I dare you to be open. To be honest. To confront the parts of yourself you've ignored. To believe that no matter where you've come from, you can be healed. You can be whole. You can be unbreakable. We are not writing this book for applause; we are writing it for alignment. This is your invitation. Your turning point. Your call to rise.

Answering the Call

I've always believed that when purpose calls, it rarely does so quietly. It shows up in whispers and waves, nudging you, stretching you, sometimes overwhelming you, but never without intention. When Joseph Gause called and said, "Tameika, I need you to direct this next course," I didn't just hear his voice; I also felt God's presence. For a split second, I froze, not out of fear but out of reverence. I knew what I was being asked to carry.

This wasn't just a leadership opportunity; it was a divine assignment, an oil-soaked mantle to steward the hearts and healing of women who, like me, had been broken, buried, and dismissed but were still breathing. If you're still breathing, you're still becoming. I didn't say "yes" right away, not because I didn't want it, but because I needed to count the cost. I took it to prayer. I searched my spirit. I asked the Father, "Is this mine to carry?" And just like that, He reminded me: You don't go where you are not graced to grow.

My "yes" came from a place of both obedience and urgency. I could feel the assignment pushing at my chest, reminding me that this wasn't about me; it was about every woman who was waiting for someone bold enough to show up, to set the standard, to say, "I'm not here to babysit your pain. I'm here to birth your breakthrough." Answering the call meant shifting from being the one who needed healing to the one who had to hold space for it, and that's not glamorous. It meant dying to ego, it meant canceling distractions, it meant carrying the emotional weight of women I hadn't even met yet. It meant setting boundaries with people who wouldn't understand why I suddenly had less time for conversations that didn't match the weight of my purpose. It meant becoming the example I wanted these women to follow, not perfectly but passionately; not with perfection, but with presence.

Directing Unbreakable Woman meant I had to live what I was taught before I ever taught it. So, I began preparing my heart, mind, and space. I cleaned my environment, both physically and spiritually. I wrote outlines. I cast vision. I prayed over every session, every topic, every woman who would log into that Zoom room. I asked God to send the right ones and to remove those who weren't ready. This wasn't a popularity contest. It was a purposeful confrontation. When the names started rolling in and the class began to fill, I felt that familiar mix of humility and fire. These women weren't just signing up for a class; they were stepping into a collision with destiny.

I knew I had to be ready. Answering the call also meant I had to challenge the modern mindset of what growth looks like. Healing isn't always soft and poetic. Sometimes, it's raw; sometimes, it's loud; sometimes, it's exhausting. There were days when these women hated me. I accepted that. Because I wasn't called to be their friend, I was called to be their midwife. Midwives don't get scared when the labor gets loud. There were nights I cried after class, not because I was tired but because I felt the weight of each breakthrough. I saw myself in them, the girl who once felt lost, broken, and overlooked. Now, I was on the other side of the fire, helping to pull others through. That's what answering the call does: it turns your scars into strategy.

The truth is, I could have said no. I could have stayed where it was safe. But something in my spirit wouldn't let me settle. Because when you know God has appointed you for something, you also know He will equip you for it. He did. He gave me the words. The discipline. The divine downloads. The emotional stamina. The boldness to call women higher and the sensitivity to hold them when they broke down. Answering the call is never just about you. It's about who you're called to impact, who you're called to cover, and who you're called to set free by simply living free yourself.

So, I showed up. Not as a perfect woman. But as a prepared one. Not with all the answers. But with all the faith. If you're reading this right now, it's because that "yes" echoed far enough to reach you. So let me say this to your spirit: When your call comes, don't run from it. Run toward it. Answer with a full heart. Answer with intention. Because someone's healing is connected to your obedience. I am proof of what happens when you say "yes" to purpose. Now, let's continue this journey together.

Only the Committed Will Survive

Before we ever opened the Zoom room, before the introductions and the icebreakers, I made something crystal clear: This is not a game. This is war. In war, you don't survive on motivation; you survive on discipline. From the very beginning, I set the standard. This wasn't your average empowerment session; this wasn't a feel-good space filled with soft words and empty affirmations. This was a spiritual boot camp for women ready to confront their pain, uproot their excuses, and reclaim the pieces of themselves they had buried to function.

I let them know plainly: If you're not going to show up for yourself every single day, don't even bother logging in. Not because I didn't love them, but because I did. Love doesn't enable you; love equips you. To equip these women meant providing them with structure, not just coddling them. That's why we had rules. Real ones. No fast food because if you want to live healed, you can't keep feeding yourself like you're still broken. No social media, except for our private group, because if you really want change, you have to silence the noise and sit with yourself. No excuses because every excuse is fear in disguise. No late arrivals, no half-effort, no disappearing when it gets hard. No quitting because if you can survive your past, you can survive your process.

We committed to meditation before sunrise. We committed to movement at least 90 minutes a day. We committed to cooking our own meals, not because it was easy, but because discipline grows in the details. We committed to journaling daily to speak to the pain, not suppress it. Every woman had to show up as if her life depended on it because, for many of them, it did. This wasn't about perfect attendance; it was about perfecting self-accountability. If you couldn't be counted on to wake up early, nourish your body, reflect on your emotions, and face the class with honesty, you weren't ready for the next level. That's okay, but we don't coddle unreadiness here; we release it.

Every requirement had a purpose behind it. We weren't just exercising to lose weight; we were shedding heaviness. We weren't journaling just to write; we were excavating trauma. We weren't logging on just to attend; we were showing up for war and winning. The truth is, I didn't design the program to be comfortable. I designed it to be confrontational because healing will never take place in a comfort zone.

These women had spent years surviving without a structured life. Years numbing themselves with chaos, inconsistency, and people-pleasing. They had performed strength for others while secretly bleeding inside. This course stripped all of that away. There was nowhere to hide. For the first time, many of them saw themselves unmasked and unedited. Some didn't make it. Some couldn't handle the pressure. Though it broke my heart to see them go, I knew what I had to protect.

The integrity of this space could not be compromised, not even by good intentions, because good intentions won't keep you whole; commitment will. We weren't building temporary results; we were building Unbreakable Women. Unbreakable doesn't mean untouched; it means tested and still standing. There were nights I could feel the fatigue in their eyes. I knew the internal battle they were facing. I saw the silent wars, the temptation to retreat, the pressure to run, the lies whispering, "You're not strong enough." I also saw something else rise: fire. I saw the woman who wanted to quit and stay another day. I saw the one who showed up late decide never to do it again.

Some couldn't even pray when they came in. Not because they didn't believe, but because they were angry at God, at themselves, and at life. Instead of condemning them, we made room for it. Because part of healing is telling the truth about where you are, even when it's messy, even when you're mad at the God you're praying to. We didn't run from those confessions; we welcomed them because this wasn't a course for perfection, but a course for resurrection.

I'll never forget one woman's story, a mother of four, living in silence with a man who no longer saw her. Who hadn't heard her voice in years, not because she wasn't speaking, but because he'd tuned her out. The worst part was that she had, too. She had forgotten what it meant to feel. She functioned on autopilot, cooking, cleaning, working, and managing to survive. She never complained because somewhere in her mind, the struggle had become a sign of loyalty. One night, something cracked. The woman who hadn't cried in over ten years wept. Not because she was weak but because she had finally given herself permission to matter.

That's what the rose does; it doesn't just bloom, it pierces. It breaks through the concrete, yes, but it also reclaims its space, its color, its softness, and its strength. That's what we were becoming. Not women who had it all together, but women brave enough to break open. We didn't just talk about the pain. We processed it. We didn't just mention the trauma. We sat in it. We didn't just acknowledge the past. We pulled it out by the root. This was the beginning of becoming.

I want to pause here to honor every woman who chose to stay. Who chose to keep showing up? Who decided to say, "I deserve to heal. I deserve to be seen. I deserve to rise. You are not a product of your environment. You are a living example that even in the most challenging places, beauty can still flourish. And this? This is just the beginning of your bloom. "What You Sold Your Purpose For, Was It Worth It?" This was the night that made some of them want to quit.

Not because they weren't strong, but because the truth hit too close. We asked the question out loud and let the weight of it settle into the atmosphere: "What did you sell your purpose for? Was it worth it?" That question didn't come gently. It came like a gut punch, and it needed to. Because for so long, many of us traded the promise of who we were for the comfort of who others required us to be. We shrunk. We settled.

We silenced ourselves. We laid down our gifts, our dreams, and our convictions just to be chosen, to belong, just to keep the peace. Some traded purposes for a paycheck. Some traded it for a man. Some traded it for a title. Some traded it for silence so they wouldn't rock the boat or be perceived as being "too much." When we finally paused long enough to look around, we realized we were living lives that didn't even feel like our own. The assignments we were born to carry were sitting on shelves collecting dust while we kept pretending we were fulfilled. But deep down, we knew we had made an exchange.

Now, it was time to take inventory. This night wasn't about shame. It was about recognition. Because what you don't recognize, you can't repent for. And what you don't repent for, you won't change. What you won't change will keep you bound. We opened our journals, and we got honest. We listed every decision we made that moved us further from who we were created to be. The relationships, the lies, the fears, the compromises, the denial, and the comfort. As the list grew, so did the revelation: Purpose isn't lost; it's misplaced. Anything misplaced can be reclaimed. But only if you're willing to confront the truth. We did, we sat in silence, we wept, we shook. We breathed through the discomfort. Because the truth will always cost you something, but it will never cost you more than staying stuck.

We asked hard questions: Who told you that was love? Who convinced you that you had to shrink to be safe? Who made you believe you had to earn what God already gave you? Why did you choose them over you? Why did you settle there? Why did you stay? And for the first time, many of the women didn't run from the answers. They wrote until their hands hurt. They cried until their faces swelled. They forgave themselves out loud. And something miraculous happened. They began to take their power back. Not in a loud, performative way. But in a sacred, grounded, unapologetic way. They started saying "no" with their chest. They started remembering what it felt like to dream. They started walking taller, speaking clearly, and showing up fuller.

When you realize what you gave up and how much of your life was spent grieving what you didn't fight for, you stop playing with your potential. You start guarding it like your life depends on it. Because it does, this wasn't just a class session. It was a funeral for the lies. A burial of the old version. A eulogy for the excuses. And in its place? Purpose began to rise again. I'll ask you, too, since you're reading this: What did you sell your purpose for? And now that you've named it. Are you ready to buy it back? Because redemption is always on the table. But only for the willing.

`What's On Your Plate?

It's not always what we're eating that's weighing us down. Sometimes, it's what we're carrying. That's the heart behind this chapter, behind the class that changed how we saw our own lives. "What's On Your Plate?" wasn't about food, though we used it as the metaphor. It was about capacity. Priorities. Self-neglect. It was about realizing that many of us were spiritually malnourished, not because we didn't have access to nourishment, but because we kept feeding everyone else first. And by the time we sat down to our portion, there was nothing left.

We were doing too much for too many, with too little left over for ourselves. Some of us had plates full of responsibilities we didn't even ask for. We inherited trauma. We carried our family's secrets. We became emotional dumpsters for friends who never reciprocated. We became the strong one, the go-to, the dependable one. In doing so, we stopped being women; we became machines. Unbreakable Woman forced us to slow down and take inventory. What was on your plate that didn't belong to you? What were you consuming that didn't nourish you? What did you agree to out of guilt instead of grace? We wrote it all down.

Some women discovered their plate was piled high with obligations that came from people-pleasing. Others found theirs was full of distractions, things that looked good but weren't God. Some women realized they had been fasting from self-worth while feasting on validation. And the thing is, none of it was sustainable eventually; an overloaded plate breaks. We had to learn how to say no. Not because we were being selfish, but because we were finally practicing stewardship. Stewardship over our energy, stewardship over our time. Stewardship over our calling. And that kind of stewardship requires boundaries. Healthy ones. Clear ones. Loud ones, if necessary.

We had to relearn how to rest. Not just sleep, but rest. The kind of rest that lets your spirit breathe. That reminds you that you don't have to earn your worth by overextending yourself for people who wouldn't even miss a meal for you. We made a declaration in that class: If it's not aligned with my assignment, it doesn't get a seat at my table. And we meant it. Because too many of us had been starving ourselves of peace, of purpose, of presence, trying to keep people fed who never intended to stay.

That night, we took our plates back. We removed what didn't serve us. We repented for how we neglected ourselves. We recommitted to eating the fruit of our purpose. We made room for nourishment again. So, I ask you today: What's on your plate? Is it feeding your soul or just filling your time? Because you can't keep running on empty and calling it strength. It's time to refill. It's time to choose yourself without apology. It's time to eat from the table God prepared for you. And not everyone gets a seat.

What Are You Afraid Of?

Fear is a liar. But before we can call it that, we have to face it. This chapter was one of the most emotional nights of the course, not because we discovered something new but because we finally looked at what we had been trying to ignore for years. We called it out and put it all on the table: fear of failure, fear of success, fear of rejection, fear of being alone, fear of not being enough, fear of being too much, fear of outgrowing the people we love, fear of starting over, fear of being seen, fear of being forgotten. So many fears. So many lies. And we were tired of being held hostage by them.

One by one, the women began to speak their fears aloud. For some, it was the first time they had ever given language to what had been tormenting them in silence. For others, it was like pulling the covers off a monster they now realized was made of paper. Fear only has power in the dark. Once you bring it into the light, it shrinks. We didn't dismiss the fears. We examined them. Where did they come from? Who told you that you couldn't? What failure convinced you that you weren't worthy to try again? What voice are you still obeying that isn't even God? And slowly, the walls started to fall. Because fear will disguise itself as wisdom, it'll dress up like discernment. It'll pretend to be humility.

But it's none of those things. Fear is bondage in a beautiful dress. We had to tear it off. And we did, with truth. We held up God's promises like a mirror and watched the lies fall apart. We opened journals and wrote down every fear, then crossed each one out with declarations. We shouted over the silence. We danced in defiance of the chains. We prayed like warriors, not begging but commanding. Because freedom isn't something you hope for. It's something to fight for.

We fought that night. We fought for the girl who was scared to speak. We fought for the woman who still thinks she's unworthy. We fought for the mother who hadn't taken a breath without fear in over a decade. We fought for the leader who secretly doubts herself. We fought for each other. As we fought, we remembered: You can't be both fearful and faithful. You have to choose. We chose faith. And that choice changed everything. So now I'll ask you, yes, you: What are you afraid of? And more importantly, what would your life look like if you weren't? Because the moment you stop feeding fear, you start living again. And Unbreakable Women? We don't bow to fear. We break it.

What Dulled Your Shine?

She didn't even realize it was gone. That was the hardest part. Somewhere along the way, life dimmed her light, and she got used to it. She adapted to the shadows. She learned how to function without fire. She forgot that she used to sparkle when she walked into a room, that her laugh used to be louder, her joy used to be fuller. This chapter wasn't about becoming someone new. It was about remembering who you were before life made you forget. "What Dulled Your Shine?" forced us to ask the questions we often avoid: When did you stop glowing? Who made you feel like your light was too much? That moment convinced you that being invisible was safer than being radiant? This night, we pulled out mirrors, not physical ones, but emotional and spiritual ones. We held them up to our inner child, our teenage selves, our twenty-something versions that still existed under the surface. And what we saw broke us.

We saw the moments when we decided to dim. For some, it was rejection from a parent. For others, it was betrayal in a relationship. Some women recalled being perceived as too loud, too expressive, and too powerful, and being punished for it. So, they learned to mute their magic. To lower their voice. To sit small, to ask for less. To take up less space. However, the truth is that God never asked us to shrink. He called us to shine. And that shine? It's not arrogance. It's alignment. When you're walking in who you truly are, it radiates. Not because you're trying to be seen, but because light can't help but shine.

So, we did the work, we traced the pain, we wrote letters to the little girl in us who stopped dancing. We repented for abandoning her. We promised to protect her now. We stood in the mirror, literally, and reminded ourselves what glory looked like. And piece by piece, the light returned. I watched women smile for the first time in weeks. I saw them wear color again. I saw them show up to class with their cameras on, no longer hiding behind black screens and broken confidence. Something had shifted. Because once you realize your shine was never really lost, just buried, you'll start digging for it like your life depends on it. And it does.

Your radiance is part of your calling. Your glow is your assignment. Your joy is your weapon. Unbreakable Women don't apologize for the light; we protect it. We polish it. We let it lead. So now I ask you: What dulled your shine? And what are you willing to do to get it back? Because you weren't born to blend in. You were born to blaze.

Congratulations, You Made It

You made it. Not because it was easy. Not because you had all the answers. Not because life let up or pain disappeared. You made it because you refused to quit. This chapter isn't about perfection. It's about persistence. It's about the quiet moments no one saw, the tears you cried in silence, the fears you faced without applause, the journal pages filled with truths that terrified you. This journey required more than commitment. It demanded surrender. You surrendered old patterns.

You laid down your pride. You permitted yourself to grow, even when growth meant letting go. You chose to show up for yourself. And that changes everything. Because the woman who started this journey is not the same woman reading these words. You are more aware. More grounded. More aligned. More powerful. You've been forged in fire, refined by truth, and filled with purpose. And sealed with resilience, you are an Unbreakable Woman, not because you don't bend, but because you no longer break in the places that once shattered you.

This chapter is your evidence. Evidence that healing is possible. Evidence that obedience breeds elevation. Evidence that community matters. Evidence that God still uses the broken things and makes them beautiful. And now, you get to carry this with you, not just as a memory but as a mantle. The world needs what you've cultivated here. Other women need your story. Your children need your example. Your future needs your endurance.

So don't stop here. Keep journaling. Keep healing. Keep rising. Keep checking your plate. Keep guarding your glow. Keep refilling your cup. Keep choosing purpose over comfort, and most of all, keep remembering who you are. You are light. You are loved. You are necessary. You are enough. You are unbreakable, walk with your head high. Speak with authority. Love without fear. Lead with compassion. When life tries to test the woman you've become, smile gently and say. "I was built for this." Because you were. Congratulations, sis. You made it.

Tina Marie

The Power of Healing: My Journey of Self-Discovery, Strength, and Transformation

My name is Tina, and I am radiating with gratitude as I share my story with you. Life hasn't been easy; it's been filled with challenges and moments that tested my strength, often making me feel like the weight of the world was too heavy to bear. It's been a journey deeply affected by trauma and abuse, yet illuminated by healing, resilience, and transformation along the way. As I open my heart and share my story, I hope to inspire and empower you, reminding you that within each one of us lies an incredible strength capable of overcoming our circumstances. Like many of you, my journey has been filled with darkness, struggles, heartache, and pain.

Sharing my story isn't just about me; it's about the power of women not being afraid to speak their truth. So many of us carry hidden scars beneath the weight of fear and shame. I urge you to break the silence that keeps us bound to our pain. Our stories are waiting to be told. I'm telling my story, about the trauma I survived, the pain I faced, the strength to seek help and grow into the woman I was always meant to be, and the healing I am still learning to embrace. It is about believing I am worthy of a life that feels safe, whole, and free.

The Weight I Carried: A Life Shadowed by Pain
"Sometimes the heaviest burdens are the ones we carry in silence."

For many, the pain begins early. As long as I can remember, I carried the weight of my childhood like an invisible backpack, heavy yet unnoticed by most. I learned early on how to read a room, how to shrink myself to avoid conflict, and how to bottle up fear like it was a normal part of growing up. I became an expert at hiding my pain and pushing down the parts of me that ached for safety, affection, and peace. I learned that silence could be safer than speaking, and that pretending everything was okay was sometimes the only way to survive.

Trauma can manifest in different ways: physical, psychological, or emotional, leaving deep imprints on the mind and body. It can also come in many forms, like the betrayal of trust, neglect, loss of a loved one, or scars left by abuse. I never imagined that the pain I carried as a child would follow me into adulthood. For years, I carried emotional baggage, yet I struggled to let it go. Experiencing trauma in childhood often conditions individuals to accept dysfunction as normal. When love is mixed with fear, or safety is tied to silence, it becomes difficult to recognize red flags in future relationships.

Trauma is a force that can shape one's life. Societal expectations, limited beliefs, and past experiences configure our identity. Entering adulthood with unprocessed trauma served as a challenge for most of my life, and it manifested in various ways. Adulthood promised independence and adventure, yet I found myself haunted by the raw wounds of my heart that I learned to hide rather than heal. There was a time when I truly believed that love meant enduring pain. I often told myself that every tear shed was a sign of true love, as if pain were a necessary ingredient in the recipe for romance. Dysfunction was familiar; unfortunately, familiarity often feels like home, even when painful.

Behind Closed Doors: Living with the Enemy
"Not all wounds are visible, and not all prisons have bars."

I ended up with an abusive husband who broke me in ways I didn't know were possible. I found myself in a relationship with someone who minimized me, controlled me, and eventually hurt me. At first, he was charming and affectionate. I was drawn to his charisma, but that quickly turned into control. I excused his outbursts and justified his behavior. He began isolating me from my friends, criticizing my clothing choices, and questioning my whereabouts. I chalked it up to love. I thought maybe he just cared too much. The first time he yelled at me, I cried, and he apologized, bringing me flowers. The first time he pushed me, I blamed myself. "I shouldn't have provoked him," I thought.

The lines between love and abuse were so blurred in my mind that I didn't even realize I had crossed into dangerous territory until I was drowning in it. I learned to anticipate tension, to read the room like my life depended on it, and to disappear emotionally whenever things got bad. Every day, I felt like I was walking on glass, bracing for the next outburst, the next accusation, the next moment when he'd take his pain out on me. Still, I stayed because I was scared. After all, I didn't know how to leave, because I had nowhere to go, because I had children, and that's what married people do, right? They stay, for better or worse. I had become so numb, so used to the emotional rollercoaster, that I stopped recognizing the woman I once was. I was going through the motions of life, but I wasn't living. I didn't learn boundaries. I learned survival.

The Breaking Point: A Whisper That Changed Everything

"Sometimes your rock bottom whispers louder than your highest hopes."

Over time, the weight of the relationship became unbearable. Each passing day became a burden, like a heavy anchor dragging me down. It wasn't until I found myself emotionally and physically exhausted, barely recognizing the person I had become, that I realized something had to change. One night, after a particularly volatile fight, I locked myself in the bathroom. I slid to the floor, sobbing uncontrollably, bruises on my arms, a hollow look in my eyes, my spirit broken, and I heard a voice inside me say, "This is not the life you and your children deserve." That voice was my breaking point and my breakthrough. I knew I couldn't keep living like that. I knew I had to find help, even if it terrified me. That was the moment I decided to reclaim my life.

Letting Go to Rise: Releasing the Guilt, Reclaiming My Worth
"Letting go isn't weakness, it's the beginning of your comeback."

Letting go was not a single moment; it was a series of choices, again and again. It's one of the hardest parts of healing. Letting go without closure is disheartening, unjust, and unfair, so it has always been challenging. It meant accepting an apology I never received, forgiving myself for staying, and for the mistakes I made when fear dictated my choices. It meant releasing the guilt I felt for not recognizing the abuse sooner, for the times I returned after he promised to change, and for the version of me that clung to hope when there was none. It meant acknowledging that I was doing the best I could with what I had, and now that I had more knowledge, more strength, I could choose differently.

I let go of the illusion that I could fix him. I let go of the belief that love was supposed to hurt. I let go of the identity I built around being a survivor and started embracing what it meant to be a thriver. I believe that what defines us is not our survival, but our ability to thrive in the aftermath of adversity. I opened my heart to the possibility of change, which freed me from the emotional burdens that drained my energy and left me feeling powerless. Letting go gave me space to breathe, rebuild, and love myself in a way I never thought possible.

Surviving domestic abuse as an adult can feel like reliving that same helplessness from the past. However, choosing to break free from this cycle takes immense courage. It means acknowledging the past, facing painful truths, and rejecting the patterns that once felt like home. Seeking help through therapy, support groups, or trusted confidants is a powerful act of self-liberation. It marks the beginning of healing, where survival transforms into growth, and wounds begin to close. Healing became my responsibility. I realized that while I may not have caused the trauma, it was up to me to stop it from controlling my life.

Asking for help was the hardest thing I've ever done. It felt like admitting failure, like exposing a secret I had tried to keep hidden for so long. But it was also the bravest thing I've ever done. I reached out for help, not because I was strong, but because I was finally tired of being broken. Asking for help isn't surrender. It's the bravest act of self-rescue.

The Warrior Awakens: From Numbness to Purpose
"A warrior doesn't emerge unscarred; she emerges unstoppable."

I was not born unbreakable. I was carved by pain and tested by storms; little did I know that those storms would lead me to discover an unbreakable, unshakable version of myself. Trauma had a way of silencing me, making me believe I was powerless and broken beyond repair. It was a burden I carried silently, leaving scars on my soul and spirit. It struck my life like a lightning bolt, shattering my sense of self and leaving me feeling lost, isolated, and confused.

My pain held me captive for years. I carried around guilt, shame, fear, and self-doubt. I was in survival mode, enduring life, rather than truly living it. Every day, I wore a mask, pretending I was fine, while inside I was falling apart. I thought if I pretended hard enough, I would actually believe it. I felt trapped in a cycle of despair, often questioning my strength. Could I ever feel whole again? I thought I was strong because I kept pushing forward, but the truth is I was running away from my emotions. Ignoring my pain didn't make it go away; it just prolonged my suffering.

I wanted something more out of life, a profound change that would shake me from my stagnation and allow me to connect more deeply with my true self. After scrolling through endless posts about healing and reading countless books on self-empowerment, I realized I needed to pursue a structured approach to guided healing that would challenge me to face my fears, process my emotions, and rebuild myself from the inside out.

Transformation in Motion: The Beauty of Becoming
"Healing isn't a destination; it's a revolution of self."

One day, while lost in thought, I caught a glimpse of myself in the mirror. I looked different. I smiled, and for the first time, I no longer saw a broken woman but a warrior ready to rise. I had a resilient spirit that had been buried deep beneath the scars. I decided enough was enough. No more living in survival mode, no more people-pleasing, no more being the person who accepts less to make others feel comfortable.

Healing was no longer a choice; it was a necessity. A commitment to myself, the life I deserved, and the freedom I never knew I could have. It's often messy, uncomfortable, and gut-wrenching. Healing is a continuous process that takes time, self-compassion, patience, and perseverance. It requires embracing change, letting go of old patterns, beliefs, and behaviors. It wasn't just about letting go; it was about reclaiming the lost parts of myself. It's a process of breaking, releasing, renewing, and rebuilding. It's a way to restore balance and wholeness after experiencing pain. I was determined to reclaim my life, identity, and power. I relentlessly pursued healing, happiness, and the life I was meant to live.

A Course in Courage: My Commitment to Healing and Growth

"Growth doesn't come when it's easy. It comes when it's necessary."

Before enrolling in this life-changing course, I felt overwhelmed by turmoil and stuck in a cycle of emotional distress; it was a continuous pattern of burnout and dissociation. I ignored my wounds, hoping time would heal them. Oh, how I was wrong! I realized that true healing requires a conscious, consistent effort and commitment to inner work, so I decided to embark on a path of self-discovery through a six-week healing and self-development course. This course offered a framework for resilience, inner strength, mental well-being, mindset shifts, and emotional healing.

When I entered this course, it marked a turning point in my life. I knew I needed to heal, I needed to release the past instead of carrying it with me. This would allow me to dive deeper into my healing journey and reshape my life with intention and purpose. I finally decided to put myself first. Initially, I had no idea how to do that. Prioritizing myself felt selfish because we live in a world where society emphasizes self-sacrifice and people-pleasing. This made me uncomfortably guilty. It wasn't easy, but I knew this was the only way forward.

Reclaiming My Power: Boundaries, Belief, and Bravery
"Power returns the moment you stop asking for permission to exist."

The course provided me with essential tools and invaluable lessons to face adversity with strength and confidence, enabling me to confront my pain without it consuming me. I learned to embrace discomfort instead of running from it. Through daily habits that supported my well-being, such as meditation, journaling, prayer, healthy nutrition, reading, gratitude, and exercise, I began to evolve. Each time I spoke my truth, I felt a layer of pain lifting away, allowing me to persevere with courage, grace, and resilience. There were moments of progress, followed by setbacks, but also breakthroughs. Some days, I felt empowered, and others, I felt overwhelmed; regardless of how I felt, I showed up for myself every day. I realized that setbacks are not failures but stepping stones for growth.

I was led through powerful exercises and guided reflection that made me confront my wounds. By embracing this approach, I was able to release past pain and open up a new chapter of personal growth. Once I acknowledged my pain, I learned to forgive myself, and I truly began to heal. I felt a sense of peace, empowerment, and clarity as I progressed. I began to trust myself again and honor my worth.

I've been taught to manage my emotions healthily, identify my triggers, and respond with understanding. I learned to stand in my power, face life's challenges with courage, and speak up even when my voice trembles. Feedback from the instructors and mentors provided me with a clear perspective on my strengths and areas for growth.

The Power of Sisterhood: Healing in Community
"Alone we survive. Together, we rise."

I found a sisterhood of survivors who walked a similar path, in a safe space where we could express our struggles and pain without judgment. We participated in classes that focused on self-love, boundaries, mindfulness, and the importance of prioritizing ourselves without guilt. I found strength in this community of shared stories, creative expression, collective healing, and genuine connection. Every scar told a story of survival. Each of these practices helped me reconnect with the parts of myself I became dissociated from, and each session spoke to my soul.

The Eulogy of My Old Self: Burying Who I Used to Be
"To become who you were meant to be, you must let go of who you used to be."

One of the most impactful exercises was writing my eulogy. At first, the idea seemed morbid. Why on earth would I want to write about my death? However, I realized this exercise was about celebrating life, not grieving death. It forced me to confront how I lived, what I wanted to be remembered for, and the legacy I wished to leave behind. I mourned the version of myself that carried past wounds. It was an extremely emotional and eye-opening experience.

Divorcing the Past: Releasing the Woman Who Settled
"I didn't leave her behind. I honored her by choosing something better."

Another transformative moment came from a symbolic divorce from my old self. I severed ties with my doubts, fears, and unhealthy patterns that no longer served me. I divorced the woman who had tolerated less than she deserved, ignored red flags, and neglected her own needs. The old me was built for survival, but the new me is built for so much more. I let her go with love and compassion, making space for the fearless woman I was meant to become.

Giving Back the Pain: Finding Closure Without an Apology
"Closure doesn't require an apology. It requires your decision to heal."

I experienced another empowering lesson in writing a letter to my abuser, giving back my pain. This was so liberating. I could express my feelings without interruptions; no yelling, cursing, belittling, gaslighting, or violence. For the first time, my voice was invincible and could not be silenced. I finally found closure after years of abuse and an apology I never received. This was a pivotal moment in my transformation, as I reclaimed my power.

Shattered Reflections: Rebuilding From Within
"I embraced my newfound identity with confidence."

Through these deeply personal experiences, I found emotional freedom. The weight of my past no longer held me back. I emerged as a stronger, wiser, more resilient version of myself. I still have moments of grief, grief for the years I lost, the pain I endured, and the innocence I never got to keep. I visit those moments only to remind myself how far I've come.

This was more than just a course; it was a catalyst for profound transformation. It was a profoundly transformative experience that reshaped my life and enhanced my ability to overcome obstacles, enabling me to lead a fulfilled life aligned with my purpose. This course has changed my life in ways I never thought possible. It helped me accept the impact of my trauma and release my pain without fear of judgment, permitting me to process my emotions and recognize the areas I still needed to heal. I am now comfortable disconnecting from people and situations that no longer serve me or align with my purpose.

Reflecting on my journey, it has been a rich experience filled with growth, self-discovery, wisdom, and strength. It has allowed me to step into a more authentic life, fully embracing my potential. Through structured lessons, reflective exercises, and a supportive environment, I was able to heal, rebuild, and thrive. I now possess the tools and mindset to navigate life's struggles with confidence. This was more than an educational experience; it was a significant chapter in my life.

By the end of the course, I had undergone a profound evolution. I gained valuable insights into my authentic self. I no longer saw my trauma as a shameful burden; instead, I embraced it as a part of my story. My courage, resilience, and determination changed my perspective, allowing me to embrace each day with a renewed sense of purpose. This experience was not just about healing the past but about opening up to life's endless possibilities.

This journey has shown me that healing wasn't about erasing the past but about honoring its lessons and choosing to move forward with grace. It is not about reaching a final destination, but about continuously evolving. Life is a constant cycle of change; therefore, learning is a continuous process. Continue your self-improvement by exposing yourself to new experiences, reading self-development books, taking self-empowerment courses, and seeking mentorships. Navigate life with intention and live your life with purpose.

Survival to Self-Liberation: Breaking the Cycle and Reclaiming Life

"Within you lies the same fire that forged me; unbreakable, unshakeable, and free."

Healing has several stages and doesn't happen overnight. In fact, at first, it felt impossible. I had spent so long surviving that I didn't know how to exist without fear. Some days, the pain was unbearable, and I often wondered if I was making progress. It's easy to become discouraged when faced with adversity, but we are taught to draw strength and resilience from these moments.

Step by step, I began to peel back the layers of pain I had buried for years. Therapy helped me confront the little girl inside me who never felt safe, and the woman who thought she had to settle for suffering. I started journaling, crying through the pages until the words turned from sorrow to strength. I surrounded myself with people who reminded me of my worth when I couldn't see it for myself. One day, everything began to shift. I was no longer trying to heal; I was doing it.

I woke up and realized I'm not the same person I used to be. I no longer looked for closure, entertained toxic people, or overexplained my boundaries. I said no without apologizing. I chose peace over chaos because I prioritized my well-being. Healing isn't about looking better; it's about feeling better and being genuinely happy. It's not just about moving forward; it's about releasing what no longer serves us.

Looking back, I realize that every tear, breakdown, and "why me?" moment was shaping me into the unstoppable powerhouse I was always meant to be. I became a woman who values herself deeply and chooses herself every time. I am no longer surviving; I am thriving, and it feels amazing. I am beginning to live again for the first time in my life. I own my story, every scar, every lesson. The version of me that fought so hard to survive is the one who built the unbreakable woman I am today. Healing is a journey worth taking. It's a story where every chapter has new lessons and insight. It leads to the most beautiful destination: self-love.

Living Out Loud: Embodying Freedom, Joy, and Wholeness
"Healing doesn't just restore you; it sets your soul on fire."

The core of being an unbreakable woman is an unshakable self-confidence. Becoming unbreakable is a journey of self-discovery, healing, resilience, and perseverance. It requires confronting pain, reclaiming power, and embracing growth. It's about bending but not breaking, and rising stronger with every challenge, with determination and grace. She embodies courage and emotional fortitude, and she is rooted in self-love and self-awareness. She has a deep commitment to her worth, values, and purpose. She's a role model and paves the way for others. She pursues life passionately and fearlessly. She is unstoppable.

Thriving Beyond Trauma: The Rise of the Unbreakable Woman

"I am not what happened to me. I am what I chose to become."

Life is a journey filled with challenges, setbacks, and opportunities for transformation. I am no longer the woman who felt powerless, voiceless, or stuck. I am no longer the little girl who internalized fear as love. I am a woman who survived trauma and chose to heal. I still have work to do, but I face the future with open eyes and a strong heart.

I know now that I deserve peace. I deserve joy. I deserve a life that feels safe. Today, I proudly stand tall, unstoppable, and unbreakable. I am proof that no matter how deeply you've been hurt, you can rise stronger than before. I am a testament to the incredible power of healing, resilience, strength, and a symbol of hope, empathy, courage, and love. I am a warrior! I am a survivor! I am an unbreakable woman!

The Legacy of Resilience: Leading with Love and Light

"Be the woman who turns her pain into purpose and her story into strength."

I have come to understand the importance of lifting others as I rise. As unbreakable women, we are responsible for sharing our stories and inspiring those who feel stuck in the darkness. Let us create a legacy of empowerment, where every woman feels seen, heard, and valued on her journey. Let's acknowledge their trauma and celebrate their healing. The world needs more unbreakable, unstoppable, unapologetically powerful women. Your story matters. Let us rise not just as individuals, but as a collective force of extraordinary, unbreakable women, in pursuit of healing, love, and happiness.

From Silence to Strength: Speaking Truth Without Fear
"Your voice is your power. Don't let anyone turn down the volume."

This journey has taught me that asking for help is not a sign of weakness, but a sign of strength. That letting go does not mean forgetting; it means choosing freedom, and that healing is possible, even after the deepest wounds. I learned that consistency, discipline, and accountability turn aspirations into reality. I share my story because someone else might see themselves in my words and find the courage to seek their healing. I believe, with every fiber of my being, that no one is ever too broken to begin to live their life again, no one is ever too lost to be found, and it's never too late to start again.

This message is for the survivors, the warriors. The women are still finding their way to anyone who has ever felt voiceless, powerless, or unworthy. To anyone who feels lost, broken, or stuck, I want to remind you that you are not alone. There is hope, and healing is possible. Each one of us has a unique purpose. A mission that brings fulfillment and meaning, so embrace your journey, however messy or chaotic it may be, knowing that every twist and turn is shaping you into the incredible person you are destined to be. You are so much more than your trauma; your transformation is within reach. Undoubtedly, never underestimate the strength that lies within you. There is an unbreakable spirit within all of us. If I can emerge from the darkness, so can you. Are you ready to become unbreakable?

I want to thank my beautiful sisters for being an integral part of my journey and for allowing me the honor of being a part of yours. Your presence made a difference. Here's to our unbreakable spirits and infinite strength. Let's continue to shine!

Gratitude for the Guiding Lights: Honoring Those Who Showed the Way

"Some taught me by lifting me up. Some taught me by letting me fall. Both made me unbreakable."

I extend my heartfelt gratitude to our instructors and mentors for dedicating your time, knowledge, and wisdom to our growth. Your unwavering support has given us the incredible opportunity to strive for the best version of ourselves. Thank you for empowering us to stand up for ourselves, encouraging us to embrace new experiences, take risks, and embody courage. Your no-nonsense approach to navigating life's challenges has been invaluable. You have helped us reflect on our journeys and shown us that life is wonderful even in the darkest moments. Thank you for your encouragement, for offering us financial opportunities, and for pushing us to excel. You have taught us to be independent, powerful, and unbreakable women. I am deeply grateful to all of you.

Eleanor N. Brown

The Journey Begins

The Unbreakable Woman Challenge, the very name resonated with a yearning deep within me, a whisper of the woman I knew I could be. I was buried beneath layers of self-doubt and the ingrained habit of prioritizing everyone else's needs above my own. It wasn't a physical obstacle course or a test of endurance in the traditional sense, though it demanded a different kind of strength, the fortitude to confront the tangled landscape of my mind and heart. This was a battlefield of the soul, where the enemy was the insidious voice of self-criticism and the heavy chains of people-pleasing.

I had arrived at this juncture feeling like a faded photograph of myself, the vibrant colors leached away by years of neglect. The reflection staring back from the mirror was a stranger, her eyes holding a weariness that belied her age. I knew, with a certainty that both terrified and exhilarated me, that something had to shift. This challenge was my desperate, hopeful leap into the unknown, a chance to finally excavate the woman I was meant to be.

And then there was Joe...

He wasn't a drill sergeant barking orders, nor a guru dispensing mystical pronouncements. Joe possessed a different kind of power, a quiet strength that radiated understanding and unwavering belief in the potential of each participant. From our very first virtual meeting, his presence was a steadying force. His words weren't sugar-coated platitudes, but rather sharp, insightful truths delivered with a genuine warmth that disarmed my defenses. Joe spoke of purpose, of inherent worth, of the shackles we unknowingly forge for ourselves. It wasn't just what he said, but the conviction in his voice and the unwavering gaze that seemed to see past my carefully constructed façade, that began to stir something within me.

I remember one early session vividly. I had mumbled something about feeling selfish for wanting to prioritize my own needs. Joe's response was gentle but firm. "Self-care isn't selfish," he stated, his voice resonating with a profound understanding. "It's the very foundation upon which you build the strength to care for others authentically. You cannot pour from an empty vessel." It was a simple analogy, yet it struck me with the force of a revelation. Years of putting others first had left me depleted, resentful, and ultimately less capable of truly supporting them.

Joe's wisdom wasn't delivered in grand pronouncements, but woven into the fabric of our interactions through his thoughtful responses to our struggles, in the way he held space for our vulnerabilities, and in the unwavering belief he projected back to us. He didn't offer quick fixes or easy answers, but instead, guided us to look inward, to ask the difficult questions, and to unearth our truths. He was the catalyst, the spark that ignited a flicker of hope within the darkness I had allowed to settle around me. He showed me, not by telling, but by being. He showed me that a different life was not just a figure of my imagination or a fantasy I dream about. But a tangible possibility if I dared to step onto the path of self-discovery.

The initial days of the Unbreakable Woman's Challenge were a turbulent sea of emotions. Fear was the unwelcome passenger that sat beside me during each session, whispering insidious doubts in my ear. Can I do this? What if I fail? What if I'm not strong enough? Uncertainty clouded my vision, making the six-week journey ahead feel like an insurmountable mountain range shrouded in mist. If I'm truly honest with myself, a persistent hum of self-doubt vibrated beneath the surface. Years of minimizing my own needs had cultivated a deep-seated belief in my inadequacy. Could I, the perpetual giver, the one who always puts herself last, truly become unbreakable?

I clung to the faint glimmer of hope that Joe had ignited, the promise of a better version of myself waiting on the other side. But the path was far from easy. There were tears that streamed down my face during particularly raw self-reflection exercises, moments when the weight of past neglect felt physically crushing. My body ached from the unfamiliar demands I was beginning to place upon it, and exhaustion became a constant companion. Yet, a fierce determination began to take root. Through the emotional storms and physical discomfort, a mantra echoed in my mind: results matter. I had to push through, to wade through the discomfort, to emerge on the other side where that elusive greatness beckoned.

The pivotal moment, the undeniable crack in my self-doubt, came during Kari's class. It was an evening etched into my memory, a visceral experience that shook me to my core. The exercise was simple yet profoundly confronting. We were asked to look into a mirror, to be honest, and acknowledge the person staring back. Not the roles we played, not the expectations we carried, but the raw, unfiltered self. Kari's words that night were like a surgeon's scalpel, cutting through the layers of denial I had so carefully constructed. He spoke of the compromises we make, the dreams we abandon, the ways we allow ourselves to fade into the background. He held up a mirror not just to our physical appearance, but to the state of our minds and spirits, the neglect, the mistreatment, the slow erosion of our inherent worth.

As I gazed at my reflection that night, the years of putting others first swam before my eyes. I saw the weariness etched on my face, the slump in my shoulders that spoke of carrying burdens not my own. The dam finally broke. A wave of grief washed over me, grief for the woman I had allowed myself to become, for the potential I had suppressed, for the love I had so freely given to others while starving my soul. But during the grief, a spark ignited. Kari's words weren't accusatory; they were an invitation, a powerful call to reclaim ourselves. Something shifted within me that night, a deep and fundamental recalibration of my priorities. The voice of self-doubt began to quiet, replaced by a nascent sense of self-compassion and a fierce, unwavering resolve.

It wasn't just Kari, though his class served as the catalyst. Each instructor throughout the Unbreakable Woman's Challenge dropped invaluable "diamonds" of wisdom into my being. They challenged my limiting beliefs, encouraged my vulnerability, and celebrated my small victories. Each session chipped away at the old me, revealing a stronger, more resilient core. But that night with Kari, staring into my own eyes and hearing his powerful message, was the turning point. It was the moment I truly saw myself, not as the person I had become, but as the Unbreakable Woman I was always meant to be. The change wasn't gradual; it was a seismic shift in my mindset, a commitment to myself that would forever alter the trajectory of my life.

Life, I've come to realize, is an unpredictable journey. You never truly know the detours it will take, the unexpected encounters that will forever alter your course, or the profound lessons hidden within seemingly ordinary moments. I certainly never anticipated that a six-week challenge would unravel years of ingrained habits and reshape my very understanding of myself. For so long, I believed I was doing the "right" thing, prioritizing others, seeking their approval, and molding myself to fit their expectations. What I didn't understand was the slow erosion of my own identity, the quiet sacrifice of my own needs on the altar of people-pleasing.

The Unbreakable Woman's Challenge cracked that mold. It forced me to open my eyes and confront the uncomfortable truth: that I am, and always will be, the most important person in my life. This wasn't an act of selfishness, but a fundamental shift in perspective. I had to show up for myself, be my unwavering advocate, and stand firmly by my side. People may come and go from my life, but I remain constant. I can no longer afford to put myself on the shelf, to diminish my worth. My body, my life, my mind, these are precious gifts entrusted to my care. I am the steward of my well-being, and allowing negativity or the needs of others to consistently overshadow my own is no longer an option.

Looking back, I see how every experience and every challenge I allowed to shape me have led me to this pivotal moment. The tears, the exhaustion, and the difficult confrontations with my reflection were all part of the forging process. Today, I stand resilient, driven, and locked in on my purpose. I am someone greater than the woman I once imagined, a testament to the power of self-prioritization and the unwavering belief of others.

It was the team behind the Unbreakable Woman's Challenge, the influential individuals who had walked this path before me, who truly made this transformation possible. They saw a potential within me that I had long ignored. They took a chance, offered guidance, and ushered me into the woman I was divinely designed to be. Beyond the instructors, the sisters I gained during this journey are an unexpected and invaluable treasure. Sharing our vulnerabilities, our triumphs, and our struggles created a bond that transcends our differences.

Their stories echoed my own, a powerful reminder that I am not alone in this walk. We are a tapestry woven with unique threads, yet our fundamental desire for self-acceptance and empowerment unites us. The Unbreakable Woman's Challenge wasn't just a course; it was a rebirth, a moment when I finally permitted myself to step into my power, shed the weight of expectation, and embrace the woman I am still becoming. The journey continues, but now I walk with a newfound clarity and an unshakeable sense of self-worth. I am unbreakable, not because I am immune to challenges, but because I now possess the inner strength to face them head-on, knowing that I am worthy, capable, and enough.

Joe's understanding of the human psyche felt almost uncanny. It wasn't just surface-level motivation; it was a deep, almost primal knowing of how the world operates and the intricate ways in which we, as individuals, often sabotage our own well-being. His teachings weren't about external validation or fleeting trends; they were rooted in the fundamental truth that everything we need to be whole and successful resides within us. He spoke with an unwavering conviction that we were each created with an innate capacity for greatness, for healing, for self-reliance. "You don't need anyone to become who you are," he would often emphasize, his words like a steady drumbeat against the anxieties that gnawed at our self-esteem. "Trust that you were divinely equipped with everything necessary for your journey."

This concept was revolutionary for me. Years of seeking approval and validation outside myself had left me feeling perpetually incomplete, like a puzzle missing essential pieces. Joe's guidance began to dismantle this dependency, encouraging me to look inward, to trust my own instincts, and to recognize the inherent power within. He used numerous examples, drawn from his own life and the experiences of others, illustrating how prioritizing oneself wasn't selfish, but rather the very foundation upon which true strength and authentic connection are built.

Throughout my weight loss journey, Joe's unwavering support was a constant source of fuel. He didn't offer quick fixes or empty promises. Instead, his reminders were sharp and direct, cutting through the layers of denial I had constructed around my physical neglect. "Look at yourself," he would say, not with judgment, but with a stark honesty that jolted me. "See how you've allowed years of prioritizing others to manifest in a body that no longer serves you." These weren't easy words to hear, but they were the catalyst I desperately needed. They stripped away the excuses and forced me to confront the physical manifestation of my self-neglect.

Fueled by this directness and a growing sense of self-respect, I locked into a consistent routine. Daily exercise became non-negotiable; preparing nutritious meals was a form of self-care, and tracking my caloric intake was a mindful act of honoring my body. The results were undeniable. The weight began to shed steadily, almost effortlessly, at a rate of two pounds a week, a tangible testament to the power of consistent effort and self-trust. It was an invigorating realization that the complex, often contradictory information I had absorbed over the years about weight loss was largely unnecessary. My body knew what it needed; I had to listen and provide it with the correct fuel and movement. This journey became a powerful metaphor for my entire transformation; the answers weren't external; they were within me all along.

Kari's contributions to this transformation were equally profound, often delivered through powerful metaphors and evocative imagery. His lesson about the flower growing in the dark resonated deeply within me. Life, he explained, will inevitably present us with darkness, hardship, pain, and seemingly insurmountable obstacles. But just as a flower develops strength to push through the dirt and reach for the light, so too do we possess the resilience to grow and blossom even in the most challenging circumstances. "No matter how dark it gets, no matter how deep the dirt, you have the potential to emerge as something beautiful, something extraordinary," he would say, his voice imbued with a quiet strength that was deeply inspiring. "You still can shine bright, like a diamond forged under pressure."

This imagery became a powerful anchor for me. During moments of doubt or when the weight of past experiences threatened to pull me back, I would recall the image of that tenacious flower. It reminded me that my current struggles were not an endpoint but an opportunity for growth, a testament to my inner strength. It fostered a deeper trust in the process, even when the path ahead seemed unclear. It nurtured a burgeoning belief in my resilience, a quiet knowing that I could not only survive but thrive, regardless of the darkness I had encountered.

The bond that formed with the other women in the Unbreakable Woman's Challenge was an unexpected and deeply cherished aspect of this journey. We arrived as individuals, each carrying our unique burdens and vulnerabilities. But through shared experiences, raw honesty, and unwavering support, we transformed into a sisterhood. When one of us faltered, we all felt it. We rallied around her, offering encouragement, understanding, and unwavering love. We celebrated each other's victories, no matter how small, and held space for each other's pain.

The obstacles we faced during the course, both individually and collectively, became unexpected catalysts for growth. They reminded us of our shared humanity, our inherent strength, and the importance of leaning on one another. These challenges forged a powerful sense of camaraderie, reinforcing the understanding that we were not alone in this journey. We learned that persevering, even when it felt impossible, was a testament to our commitment to ourselves and each other. "Nothing can stop us but us" became an unspoken mantra, a reminder of the internal power that each of us possessed.

A profound shift occurred within me regarding my worth and the energy I was willing to expend on others. I came to the powerful realization that I, above all others, deserved the very best of myself. The ingrained habit of prioritizing everyone else's needs began to feel like a betrayal of my inherent value. The desire to constantly show up for those who had consistently failed to show up for me started to dissipate. The need to be the ever-reliable support system, even at my own expense, finally broke.

I learned that it was okay to lean on myself, to be my primary source of strength and support. This wasn't about isolating myself, but about establishing a healthy sense of self-reliance. The fear of disappointing others began to pale in comparison to the growing desire to honor my own needs and boundaries. I no longer felt compelled to be overly cautious with my words or to agree with things that contradicted my sense of truth. Honesty, both with myself and with others, became a guiding principle. I discovered the liberating power of "no" as a complete sentence, free from the need for lengthy explanations or justifications, regardless of someone's title or perceived authority in my life. My convictions became my anchors, and my words aligned with my inner truth.

The transformation taking place within me was palpable. While the physical changes were noticeable, the internal shift was far more profound. Interestingly, as I began to prioritize myself and live in alignment with my values, some relationships in my life began to shift, and yes, some even dissolved. Those who had grown accustomed to the "old me", the one perpetually in service mode, the one who consistently placed their needs above her own, struggled with this newfound self-assertion. I understood that this shedding was a necessary part of my growth. Holding onto relationships that were predicated on an imbalanced dynamic would only hinder my progress.

Living in my purpose now feels like stepping into a vast, open space after being confined to a small, cramped room. It is the most liberating and authentic feeling I have ever experienced. Through daily meditation and journaling, I cultivated a deeper connection with my inner self and gained clarity on the changes that were necessary for my growth. It wasn't always easy; confronting deeply ingrained patterns and beliefs is challenging work. The desire for a more authentic and fulfilling life propelled me forward.

The chains of obligation that once bound me have been broken. I feel lighter in my spirit, no longer held down by the weight of unmet expectations and the constant need to please. My primary obligation now is to myself, to nurture my well-being, to honor my truth, and to live a life aligned with my deepest values. I want to speak directly to anyone reading this who may be grappling with self-doubt or the fear of change. Recognize that the moment those feelings surface, the moment that inner voice whispers anxieties and uncertainties, is often the very indication that you are on the right path. It signifies that something within you is resisting the shift, that the "old you," comfortable in its familiar patterns, is hesitant to let go. It's the part of you that has benefited from your self-neglect, the part that wants you to remain in service mode, to continue the cycle of prioritizing others at your own expense.

This resistance is a natural part of growth. It doesn't mean you're on the wrong track; it means you're challenging the status quo within yourself. Push through that discomfort. Recognize that those feelings of doubt are often the last desperate attempts of your old self to maintain control. You deserve better. You deserve to live a life of purpose and fulfillment. This is your time. This is your moment. This is your year to prioritize yourself and step into your greatness.

Forget the distractions, the fleeting trends, the voices that tell you what you should be. Focus on the one thing that truly matters: results. Act. Make those difficult choices. Embrace the discomfort of growth. Get up! You have work to do, the vital, essential work of becoming the unbreakable woman you were always meant to be.

The journey doesn't end here. Becoming unbreakable isn't a destination; it's a continuous evolution. There will be new challenges, new moments of doubt, and new opportunities for growth. The lessons I learned during the Unbreakable Woman's Challenge, the wisdom imparted by Joe and Kari, and the unwavering support of my sisters have equipped me with the tools I need to navigate these future landscapes.

I now understand that self-care is not a luxury, but a necessity, the very bedrock of my strength and resilience. Prioritizing my needs allows me to show up for others authentically, from a place of abundance rather than depletion. Setting secure and healthy boundaries is an act of self-respect, as it protects my energy and allows me to cultivate genuine connections with those who truly value me. Living in alignment with my purpose brings a sense of joy and fulfillment that I had been missing for a long time.

The woman who began the Unbreakable Woman's Challenge feels like a distant memory. She was strong in many ways, but her strength was often directed outward, at the expense of her well-being. The woman I am today is strong, both inside and out. Her resilience is rooted in self-awareness, self-compassion, and an unwavering belief in her worth. She is not afraid to say no, to prioritize her needs, and to walk her path, guided by her inner compass.

The impact of Joe, Kari, and my sisters will forever be etched in my heart. They were the catalysts, the guides, and the unwavering support system that helped me unearth the unbreakable woman within. Their belief in me, even when my own wavered, was a powerful force that propelled me forward. This experience has taught me the profound importance of surrounding oneself with people who see one's potential and encourage your growth.

Now, I move forward, not with the expectation of a life devoid of challenges, but with the unwavering confidence that I possess the inner strength to navigate whatever comes my way. I am a work in progress, constantly learning and evolving. The foundation has been laid, the unbreakable woman has emerged, and she is ready to embrace her purpose and live a life of authenticity, joy, and unwavering self-love. The journey continues, and I am finally, wholeheartedly, present for it.

The Awakening

December 2, 2024. Beep, beep, beep. It's 4:30 AM. The alarm jolts me out of sleep like a slap to the spirit. I jump up, breath catching, then remember. I'm on vacation. Not just any vacation, today is Day 1 of the Unbreakable Woman Challenge. My heart is pounding. I screenshot the time and send it to the group chat. Shaky but determined, I sit at the edge of my bed and turn on my meditation music. Twenty minutes of silence. Twenty minutes of breathing. Twenty minutes of grounding myself in the reality that I said yes to something that will either break me open or build me into something brand new.

Then the scale, I step on it, hopeful, and it read two-hundred and ninety six pounds. My heart drops. I don't even feel disappointed; I feel disgusted. My first journal entry: "I cannot believe I am up this early. I cannot believe I gained so much weight. "I'm fat as FUCK. I should lie back down.", "No, I'm pushing through." "I deserve a better me." "DAMN I'm tired, this better be worth it." My words were brutal and raw, but real. It's 5:30 AM, and now it's time to work out. I searched YouTube for Juice & Toya. "You can do this," I whisper. "Just START." Five minutes in, sweat is pouring. I feel like I'm about to die. I check my watch, seven minutes and forty-five seconds. My body is screaming, and my brain is ready to quit. But I don't. I finish. Legs shaking, arms burning, and brain fogged. Still, I finished. In that moment of stillness on the couch, as my sweat becomes my badge of honor, something awakens within me, a flicker of belief.

That flicker grows through the day. I prepped my meals, tracked my calories, stretched my limbs, drank plenty of water, and completed another thirty-minute workout. I'm aching, yes, but I'm proud. That night, I met Meika in class for the first time. I'm nervous; I don't trust women easily. I've been compared, competed against, and discarded by other women far too often. But this time, this space feels different. There's unity and purpose here. Joe, our instructor, his words like spiritual scalpels, cutting into the parts of us we buried long ago. When he started pointing out the disfigurement of our bodies without saying names, I felt exposed, triggered, and angry. I wanted to log off. I knew I was one of the ones he was talking about. I feel humiliated, but I stayed. I stayed because if I run from the truth, I'll never change, and change is why I enrolled in the course. At midnight, the class finally ended. I'm exhausted, and tomorrow is Day 2.

Solitude Sunday: Unpacking
December 8th

Sunday is Solitude Sunday. This day was different. It wasn't a workout challenge; it was a spiritual mirror. Today is my sister's birthday. She is my best friend in this world. Today, I'm not supposed to talk, text, watch TV, or connect. I'm supposed to sit in complete solitude. The pain of choosing me over a moment with her was excruciating. How do you explain solitude to someone you love? I cried; I sat in my work truck with tears falling like rain. My heart was breaking; I picked up the phone and explained everything. I told her I couldn't celebrate today, but it wasn't because I didn't love her. It was because I had to choose myself for the first time in my life, and she understood. She really understood. That moment cracked me wide open.

Solitude isn't silence, it's surrender, and it's the stripping away of every distraction until all you're left with is yourself. What I saw in that mirror wasn't pretty. I saw my patterns, my pain, and my excuses. I saw the trauma I used as a crutch, the people-pleasing I called "love," and the denial I renamed "strength." That Sunday, I didn't just unpack my baggage; I owned it, I created it, and I chose comfort over confrontation. Silence over truth, weight over wellness, but no more.

The Midpoint of My Becoming

I was in rhythm by week three, rising at 4:30 AM, meditating, journaling, sweating, and meal prepping. Suddenly, life hit again. My sister was rushed to the hospital in unbearable pain. I panicked, I cried, and I prayed. Emergency surgery, life or death. I stood in that hospital room demanding that God keep His promise. I reminded Him of His Word; I needed Him more than ever. God answered my prayers, and my sister made it. I went home emotionally drained but spiritually charged. I had every excuse to skip class, but I didn't. I logged in, and I showed up. Because if I could show up for others all these years, surely, I could show up for myself. Later that week, we wrote our eulogies. It felt insane, but I did it. I buried the old me. I laid to rest the people-pleaser, the broken woman, the version of myself who constantly poured out without ever being poured into. The next morning? I felt lighter, not just in body but in spirit. I had finally said goodbye.

I Am Becoming

Week four. I started glowing, not just from the two pounds I consistently lost every week, but from the inside out. I felt sovereign, determined, and alive. I started connecting with the other women. One beautiful, warm Latina with a kind heart. We became accountability partners. I didn't know what to expect when this journey started, but God sent me a sister when I least expected it. By week five, I had lost over twenty pounds. My skin was glowing; my posture was straighter, my energy was unstoppable, and then I was named valedictorian. Me? The same girl who was gasping after 7 minutes of a workout? The same woman who cried over missing her sister's birthday? The same soul who almost let shame stop her? Yes. Me.

Can't Stop, Won't Stop

Week six. I could taste the finish line. I was walking and thinking differently. I took myself out on a date: perfume, a pretty dress, candles, and confidence. I wasn't waiting for a man, a moment, or anyone else to validate me. I validated myself. I walked through fire and didn't burn. I bent but didn't break. I healed from things I didn't even know were wounds.

The Dawn of an Unbreakable Woman
January 6, 2025

It was the final week. Graduation was around the corner, my cap and gown had arrived, and my heart was full. Every woman in our class was glowing. We had done the work, we woke up at 4:15 AM, we did the journaling, the workouts, the mental rewiring. We dug deep, we cried, we confronted our demons and our distractions. We rose.

January 10, 2025. Graduation Day.

Butterflies in my stomach, and my family was watching on Zoom, but most importantly, I was there. Present, whole, and transformed. Twelve strangers became twelve sisters. A chain that can't be broken. Though I had to work that night, I still gave my speech, because nothing could keep me from standing in the truth of my transformation. I am no longer who I used to be. I am sovereign. I am scared. I am healed. I am loved. I am light. I am an Unbreakable Woman.

Raquel M. Breaux

Needed and Necessary

Within the past ten years, incomplete checklists, unmet goals, and unfinished tasks seemed to become a habit. The things that were truly a challenge were left undone; anything that required me to put in a little more effort seemed to be a chore. I constantly procrastinated, postponed, and tried to do everything except the things I knew I needed to complete. Don't get me wrong. I had tasks that I would complete, but they were the easy ones. Being organized and disciplined for work, Zumba© classes, or things that other people needed from me, "Oh, that was easy." However, when it came to the important things, I postponed them as if I had time.

This course came at the right time. A time that the Creator knew would be best to move me in a new direction, a direction that was beneficial to me and my purpose, was what I needed. It was the one thing that I would complete. It was difficult, uncomfortable, tedious, structured, time-consuming, strict, frustrating, exhausting (little sleep), and had lots of rules. It was necessary! For six weeks, it became my new focus. It taught me to remove distractions, become disciplined about the things that were necessary, and how to say no to the things that no longer served me. In short, it taught me to put myself first.

Between Unbreakable University and personal therapy sessions, I truly found answers to what I call "feeling stuck." I wrestled with overthinking, fear, confidence, control, and procrastination. I finally had the opportunity to see myself in a way that I had never experienced. It was pure truth. When I finally started unlocking and stating the truth, it allowed me to see into myself. Our coaches were the absolute best at getting us to see ourselves. The tools and guidance were so effective that they brought awareness to more than just my fears. I was finally discovering all of me. I realized fear paralyzed me, and my self-confidence was weak. Shame forced me into a corner and kept me silent about what I knew I needed to face. I discovered my own POWER.

This moment, this very moment of typing these words, is even a breakthrough. To speak on what I kept close to the chest, I found out would be the same thing that would set me free. I have journaled for years, but I began to adore the silence during those six weeks of journaling. Not being distracted by social media, phone conversations, listening to music, and watching movies. I could hear the Creator, and I heard myself. I am now capable of hearing like I hadn't before. Messages come to me loudly and with clarity. I no longer search long for lessons in given circumstances. I'm made aware much faster.

For a while, I tried to figure out my purpose; my purpose is to show up in the world authentically. Unbreakable

University taught me that fears, lack of self-confidence, and shame kept me from being my authentic self. A specific exercise during the course allowed me to see many of my accomplishments and how they were all connected to my authenticity. All along, I thought I hadn't done much, but our purpose and how we show up matters.

We often wonder, "How did I get to this point in my life? Why is this happening to me?" I learned that it's all a part of your story that leads us to purpose. There are certain circumstances that are there to usher us into a new mindset, discipline, self-talk, perspective, and even a new spirit. Unbreakable University is part of my story because I needed to change my life and mind to point myself to my purpose. It was a compass in the forest of my mind.

Everything I thought was wilderness was necessary, too. It brought me to this moment. There's a funny thing about what we may call wilderness. We think it is scary, strange, and difficult to find our way. Oddly, the wilderness is familiar to many. When you speak of your wilderness, there is always someone who can connect to your story of feeling lost. Often, they can relate to your encounters along your path.

My path began long ago. Just as it did for many, it started in youth. Discovering the inner child and what that child needed reveals much about ourselves. "Ha! Don't worry, I won't bore you with many details," but it's important to understand exactly why Unbreakable University was on my path and why I needed it. I grew up in a loving yet unique environment. Specifically, traveling between two households. Primarily, I resided with my great aunt and uncle (older married couple), who also raised my mother. My mother's house was the weekend house because she worked evenings for the phone company. Unfortunately, my father wasn't around much, a few appearances here and there, but not very often.

"Pay attention. This is going to go fast." I'm a teenager; at age fourteen, my great-aunt passed away due to cancer. It went so fast that I can barely recall her being sick. I started living with my mother. This is a woman that I love, yet I don't know much about her at this point because my primary residence was my great-aunt's house. Just shy of two years at my mom's house, I became pregnant with a daughter whom I would put up for adoption a few months before my seventeenth birthday. My mother questioned my decision many times. But I was certain this was what I should do, considering that I was so young and had no clue how I would raise a child. This is the decision that has stayed with me for years. I later discovered that it's what brought about my fear.

The following year, I graduated from high school and went on to college at the amazing Southern University in New Orleans. I worked for the post office during college and am proud to say I didn't have any student loans when I finally graduated. It took more than five years to graduate because I'd go to school, sit out a semester or two, and then go back. This is when I realized that my follow-through was weak and I was procrastinating.

I've always held what the Baby Boomers call a "good job" during and after college. Meanwhile, I was always interested in the arts. I've played music, danced in high school and briefly in college, and written poetry for years. I performed poetry, recorded with different artists, did community outreach, and danced in an African dance troupe for three years prior to leaving New Orleans. The things I loved dearly were great. I never had the confidence to pursue the arts. Many of my decisions were based on what was easier to do, fear, and lack of confidence.

There were times when I was concerned about what others thought of me, unsure of my decisions, sought validation within my relationships, remained in relationships longer than I should, and thought I needed to do one more thing to be great. This is a part of me that existed. Peeling back the layers of self can reveal flaws, scars, and unhealed wounds. It's necessary to see it all; just when you think you're done, something else is revealed.

Three days after my fiftieth birthday, I received the greatest gift I've ever received. I received a phone call from a strange number. I don't normally answer strange phone numbers, but this time I answered. It was a woman's voice asking me questions only I would know the answer to. She introduced herself and, in a few words, she said one thing that changed my life forever. She said, "In May of 1987...." I knew immediately why she was calling. She was searching for my daughter's mother. I was nervous, anxious, and joyous at the same time. She wanted to know if it would be okay for her to call me. My daughter called me on a video conference. We cried and smiled; it was as if we were looking in a mirror. I am blessed beyond measure. I also have four beautiful grandchildren (ages 13, 10, 6 & 14 months).

Our reconnection was divine; we needed each other equally, but for different reasons. I needed to know her because I was still aching from not knowing. She needed to know me and understand her background. Almost five years later, and it's been good. There have been bumps in the road, but honesty can be a bumpy ride. I am grateful. Every part of my journey has meaning: we learn, we let go, and we graduate. Ultimately, there is a lesson in it all. No matter how difficult, scary, or uncomfortable it may be, it is of great significance. It has a part in my story. Unbreakable University helped me to see, understand, identify, and unlock my power. The necessary part of my story proved that I am UNBREAKABLE!

Lesley Burrows

Freedom: The Ultimate Goal

As part of the first group of women to graduate from the Unbreakable University 6-week course, let me tell you, it was an experience like no other. There were highs, there were lows. I wanted to quit so many times, and honestly, there were moments I didn't think I'd make it through. From day one, this course demanded more from me than I ever expected.

The curriculum was no joke. I had no idea it would mean waking up at 4 AM, meditating, praying, working out daily, and cooking every single day, with no fast food as a fallback. After working all day, who really has the energy for that? However, we still had to push through. On top of all that, we had assignments that had to be done on time, and we still had to juggle life. Bills, work, family, everything. At that time, I was going through major marriage and family issues, and it was one of the most stressful seasons of my life.

Being in class? Whew, my emotions were all over the place. I was scared, frustrated, and angry, but I was also grateful. It felt like I was on a nonstop emotional rollercoaster. This course forced me to take a real, honest look at myself and unpack the reasons why I made so many self-sabotaging decisions that were keeping me stuck. I signed up for something I truly didn't understand. Honestly? I thought we were just going to sit around and talk about "how men ain't shit." I wasn't even fully interested in that, but I was curious about what the other women would say. Boy, was I wrong. This course was nothing like that. I hadn't done any research on the instructors; I just showed up completely unaware of what I was stepping into.

Then, the first instructor popped up on screen. A beautiful young woman named Tameika. She was poised, sharp, well put together; you could just tell she was about her business. When she spoke, her voice carried this natural authority, and you listened. She immediately broke down how the classes would go, the level of accountability she expected, and that there would be absolutely no excuses and no laziness. I instantly panicked. I thought to myself, "Oh no, what did I just get myself into?" I had my routine, and I was comfortable in it, and I wasn't looking to change. But something told me to keep listening. Something told me to see this through, and that decision? It changed everything.

The first day of class was interesting, to say the least. We were introduced to our upcoming instructors and the long list of classes we'd need to complete. Honestly, I was cool with the assignments at first. No stress there. I thought, "Okay, I got this." However, class started, and all of us ladies were introduced to a man named Joe. Now, I already knew him as Purpose, that's his name on TikTok, Purpose and Resilience.

Before I signed up for this course, I came across Joe through Priscilla the Queen Maker. They had this amazing, live conversation on YouTube. Hands down, the top three best lives I've ever watched.

When Joe (Purpose) came into class, I lit up. I smiled, ready to vibe with him like I did when I watched that live. But that smile? It didn't last long. It disappeared really quickly. I was confused. This wasn't the same man I saw with Priscilla. When he spoke, his tone hit different, cold and sharp, like he didn't care. He sounded like a straight-up military drill sergeant. Trust me, I know military; I was married to a man in the military for over 10 years. Later, I understood exactly why he came at us like that.

In that moment, Joe completely caught me off guard. Where was the Purpose I knew? This wasn't him. As the class went on, my anxiety skyrocketed. I instantly slipped back into my old high school survival mode: stay quiet, sink into the background, and don't get noticed. The fear of being called on started eating me alive. Joe demanded your best. At that time, I didn't even know what my best looked like. I was just sitting there praying, "Please, don't call on me. Please."

Embarrassment? That's my biggest fear. Feeling embarrassed makes me feel stupid and small, like I don't matter. When I feel like that, all I want to do is disappear. I made it to the end of class, success! I wasn't called on. I thought

I had successfully blended in. But just as class was about to wrap up, Joe said, "I'd like these two to stay after class." Then, I heard my name. "Oh, shit." I was caught; I couldn't hide in the corner anymore. I thought I was invisible, but Joe noticed me, my silence, my smallness, my fear.

He told me straight up, that's how predators (people) prey on women like me. I didn't want that. So, I listened, really listened. The more he spoke, the more I leaned in. What he was saying hit me in ways I didn't expect. I always thought being unseen was my strength. If nobody saw me, I couldn't get embarrassed. If I couldn't get embarrassed, I couldn't feel small, unheard, or unimportant. I thought I was protecting myself by disappearing.

Joe showed me that I wasn't winning at all. I wasn't successful at anything. I was losing, silently. When I felt embarrassed, I felt worthless. When you see yourself that way? Trust me, people see it too, and when they see it, they treat you like you don't matter. Because in their minds, "if you don't care about yourself, why should they?" As the weeks went on, a new instructor, Kauri, came into the picture. He was kind, funny, super smart, he lightened the room with his humor, but packed every class with valuable information. His classes were eye-opening, especially because he taught from a man's perspective. I truly believe women need to understand men. Then Joe and Kauri did something that changed everything:

they introduced a new class: "Ask Us Anything: From a Man's Point of View." That's when something shifted in me.

Their honesty, their openness, made me feel safe enough to finally speak up. For the first time, I raised my hand to ask a question. At the time, I was going through a separation from my husband. We weren't talking. We were still living in the same house, but it was cold and distant. I couldn't understand the way he was moving, so I asked. Geesh!!! I hated myself for asking that question. I felt the embarrassment hit me instantly, like a brick. The answers they gave me? Straight, no sugarcoating, and no fluff. Just raw truth. My first instinct was to hide, to curl up and disappear, but nope! I asked the question, so I had to stand on it. Period, and I did just that.

I tucked my emotions away and locked in. I listened. I needed to hear it, I needed to understand it, from a man's point of view, with no filters. The goal was to listen and learn, and that's exactly what I did. As the classes continued, we were introduced to a session called "What's on Your Plate." Our instructor was Bridgett. Let me tell you, she was no joke. No-nonsense, slick-mouthed, and super smart. Bridgett didn't play. Her class forced me to look at every toxic, negative thing sitting on my plate, and my life was full of it.

You see, I was carrying people I should've let go a long time ago. Why? Because they were family. Specifically, my mother. I always heard people say, "But that's your mom. You only get one mom." Those words would flood me with guilt. So, I buried how she made me feel. I stuffed it so deep inside myself that I almost believed it didn't exist.

But the truth? She made me feel unwanted. She made me feel ugly, unheard, and unloved. That was my teacher; her actions taught me to live my life through the way she viewed me. Because of that, I saw myself that way. I walked around wearing that shame, and yep, it all goes back to my number one fear: embarrassment.

Through this journey, I learned something powerful: I can love my mother from afar. Maybe, one day, we'll truly understand each other. But right now? I choose myself. These classes taught me the necessity of self-love, the kind of love that says, "You will never shrink me again." I mean that. One of the hardest classes of this entire six-week journey was the one led by Rhonda, a beautiful, pure-hearted woman. Sweet, but she took us to deep waters.

In this class, we had to write our own eulogy. "Wait, what?" That's exactly what I thought. Write my own eulogy? Like, what do I even say? How do I even begin? But somehow, I found the words. Even writing this now, I feel those emotions rising again. Tears are flowing. Because not only did we write our eulogies, but we also had to read them out loud in class.

That moment broke me. How do you say goodbye to the version of yourself you've known your whole life? I was comfortable with her. I was just starting to meet this "new me," but the old me? She was familiar. When it was my turn, I started to speak. My voice was trembling, but the words poured out anyway. I felt sick, literally. I wanted to click that little red button and exit the Zoom. Get me out of here. But no, I had to finish. I wanted to win this battle, and I did.

That wasn't the end; later that night, I got sick. I was vomiting, had cold sweats, chills, and I couldn't sleep. My body was still fighting. It was like everything toxic in me was finally coming out, and I had to feel it on the way out. It wasn't just emotional, it was physical. Eventually, I drifted off to sleep. No nightmares, just rest, a peaceful night's rest. When I woke up, I wasn't 100%, but I knew I had crossed over. I made it through.

Let me reintroduce myself: I am Lesley. The new, the improved, the Unbreakable. What a journey, what a journey. Six powerful, gut-wrenching, transformational weeks, and guess what? I completed it. Let me say that louder for the people in the back, "I COMPLETED IT!" I now know my worth. I now understand respect. I now understand sacrifice, discipline, consistency, self-love, and the beauty of motivation. Most importantly, I learned to always walk toward the Creator. This was more than a course. This was the rebirth of me.

Jade Otto

Phoenix Rising

The most impactful moments in life are when you're at that point of being unrecognizable in the mirror, aching to go back, and desperately asking why while shaking, as you're gripping your pillow, sobbing as if you clench hard enough you might be able to catch the sand of who you used to be. When you have your prescription or blade in your hand, trying to decide your fate when everything seems against you, and nothing is aligning. These moments are the climaxes, forks in the road, or spiritual earthquakes to reveal truths. They are necessary. What will you choose? What does your soul say when you're about to implode? What do you hear in the dark? Will you listen to fear, or will you listen to Spirit?

I've had many moments like these and know others who have been through the same. We are not different, and we are not alone. During the six-week challenge, I relived all my memories till this point in my life; it was unrelenting, and I wanted to give up many times, but I needed to complete this. It was imperative to my development. I habitually quit right before it gets good because of my fear of failure and success. I deserve to prove to my demons that I can follow through. That I'm worthy of greatness and not just another hopeless victim of my circumstances.

Some of my first memories were witnessing my father point a gun at my mom when I was four and watching her frantically run out the door. Being sexually abused when I was five by my cousin, and despite my father walking in, he never got me help. When I cried, he called me disgusting and said he was going to throw up. So, I never cried in front of others again. I remember when I was six, I flipped off my dad, so he grabbed a kitchen knife, ran at me, and stabbed a balloon that was right next to my face. I screamed so hard I fell silent, and my parents laughed at me. I remember the night I accidentally got drugged when I was eight years old. I got yelled at while hallucinating and threw up. I wasn't hospitalized after the terrifying incident.

I remember the silence and the relief I felt when I held the blade against my neck in my Nana's kitchen when I was 10, but I heard that whisper. It told me, "Stop" during it all. That's just the tip of the iceberg. My brain is protecting me from many others, or I'm just forgetting right now, since it's been so long since something triggered those emotions. When those battles arise, I will be ready to strike the devil down like I do every single day of my life. That's why I took the challenge; I was ready to transform again, and the universe knew and guided me.

I had to let go of mindsets, relationships, and environments holding me back. My old armor was worn and beaten. It was time to get a new set. I know who I am, my truths, and my unwavering trust in myself and Spirit. I'm Unbreakable, and being Unbreakable doesn't mean that you never break down, it doesn't mean you never cry again or stop falling. It means that you decide to get up, wipe your tears, and keep going whenever that moment happens. Face the challenges and be glad you have them. Earn your keep, don't yearn to be spoon-fed by God. Only children have that luxury, and some don't even get it. Whenever I see myself or my life falling apart, I trust it's alchemizing into something more for me.

I'm constantly dying and being reborn. It's painful yet beautiful, and I'm eternally grateful. The only reason for battle is to gain something, decide wisely what that is, and move on quickly if you know it's not for you; use discernment. Time is precious, and I appreciate everyone who has given me their time. They've helped me become who I am today, whether they were sent to knock me down or lift me up. It's all in the divine plan. Allow your ego to be split apart so your true, untainted soul can emerge from the depths. Walk like the piece of God you were meant to be. Hold your head high, my friend.

The Path to Becoming Unbreakable

I could hear the light whisper of the fan as it spun in the dark above me, slowly evaporating the small beads of sweat on top of my tired body as the heat from the bed seeped into my back. I sighed and turned over to cool myself like a dog would in summer. Absent-mindedly, I took my fingers and drew circles and X's on my flings chest as he breathed heavily after another night of quick, mediocre sex. The familiar heaviness of dissatisfaction stirred in my gut, and that persistent, annoying thought rose again: "What the fuck am I even doing with my life?" I had become a creature of comfort, the living dead. Banging on my keyboard, reading emails, and daydreaming about the shoulda, woulda, coulda. Navigating through the week just to come home to a blur of a weekend filled with daily binge-watching and endless media scrolling. Slowly, the resentment grew, for everyone, everything, and especially myself.

I lived in a place that was keeping me ill. I slept next to another miserable man-child. My body was so weak it was painful, and my Spirit so dull my vision board mocked me as the dust settled on my ignored cutout dreams. I was an addict, like most people, whether they know it or not. Just constantly scrounging around looking for a crumb or scrap of serotonin or dopamine to get through the next hour or minute, whether it was sex, food, work, or entertainment, it didn't matter.

I was a bystander in my own existence, just bitching and moaning with other third persons about the unchangeable past or imagined futures, using our shared victimhood as an excuse for inaction in the present. Eventually, after another one of these passionate, empty conversations about God-knows-what, I snapped. The resentment exploded. I hung up the phone on my fling and cried furiously with guilt, anger, and relief. I blocked everyone who mirrored the worst side of me. Again, I found myself and my puffy eyes staring into the popcorn ceiling, hoping some sort of magical "How to Get Your Shit Together" manual would fall from the sky. I felt the itch for a distraction, so I closed my weary eyes, took a long breath, and asked for guidance.

That week, "Priscilla the Queen Maker" manifested on my TikTok "FYP" was like divine intervention. I was immediately drawn in by her aura and how she spoke; I was hooked. I started watching her every day. "The Free Game," featuring Purpose and Resilience, was the first time I caught her live on YouTube. When he appeared, I was taken aback. There was something powerful about his presence; it radiated, like sunlight. Intriguing, intimidating, and rare. As I watched the Queen and King speak, I held on to every word, and the moment the Unbreakable University was mentioned, I knew I had to be in that room. This inexplicable force took over before I could even have my next thought. I immediately requested to join the six-week challenge when it emerged on the page. I signed up and waited eagerly. Shortly after, I was accepted into the group. Only a handful of people would be selected, but my spirit urged me to take a chance. My heart skipped when I received the welcome email. I was nervous and enthralled as I signed the agreement.

The first night before the challenge started, I had a dream. Tall, jagged grey cliffs surrounded me. I desperately sprinted as fast as I could between the rocks as they pierced my skin. The creature was closing in, and I was filled with overwhelming fear. When I reached the edge, I quickly turned around to a huge, ominous shadow ten stories tall, hovering over me. It then morphed into seven different shadows, each with sinister features. As I reached for my blade, I was taken aback; the shadows were tethered to my feet. I realized I was facing my sins. As I drew my sword out and jetted forward, I screamed from the depths of my being: "NO!" It all went black, and a whispering yet booming voice responded in the darkness, "You pass." I woke up to my alarm set for 4:25 a.m., and it began.

I ripped the blankets off, drowned my eyes in eyedrops, clocked in, and lit my candle to start journaling. I was exhausted, but ready to take back control. During those six weeks, I felt like a lost sailor on a raft, navigating tumultuous waves of doubt, fear, anger, and hope. I pushed through the emotional, spiritual, and physical struggle daily with nothing but my willpower, sisters, and generous, unyielding guides. I journaled until my worries, thoughts, and feelings ran off the page. Then, I sat silently or used vibrations to assist as I checked my temple from head to toe and focused my breath.

Most days, my mind shifted constantly, like the clouds in the sky or fish in a pond. I observed the noise within me. I did not attempt to control it; I simply sat and observed. We often forget we are the sky or the pond, not the things in it. Once I felt satisfied, or it was time for my next task, I threw on my shoes and scarf. The winter cold burned my nose and throat as I stepped outside. I challenged myself to walk as far as my feet could take me, and that ended up being five miles every day, plus or minus working out for thirty minutes to an hour. As long as I obtained my goal for the day, I thought. The nerves in my feet were burning, my ankles were swollen, and my bones and muscles ached from the sudden switch from sedentary to highly active. Slowly, I felt myself craving the gym and the peace it brought me. The feeling of progression was invigorating! I was starting to feel alive once again.

Nourishing my body wasn't new; I had dietary restrictions and knew what I needed. But I had become addicted to expensive takeout, which drained my wallet, and I was eating the same easy-to-make, boring meals repeatedly. In times of restriction, our ancestors and descendants use one tool to survive: Creativity. So, I got creative. Instead of the all-in-one delicious mush I'd grown bored of, I had time now, even if I didn't have the money. I cooked the ingredients separately, played with flavors, and enjoyed the food I made for the first time in a long while. I broke free from the "it is what it is" mindset that had kept me complacent in things I could change.

However, my greatest breakthroughs were because of our guides, Rhonda, Joseph, Tameika, Kauri, and Bridgett. Each class they taught had techniques I had heard of before, but it was different. It didn't have fluff; it wasn't another bullshit self-help course full of superficial clapping and thumbs-ups for doing the bare minimum amount of effort. It's real, and they were serious. They would call you out, expose you, test you, teach you, and love you enough to believe you can be better. It was both terrifying and rejuvenating.

During the first week of class, I was sobbing, choking up, and having a hard time speaking through the pain of the past. I felt like a block of unfinished marble being struck with chisels and hammers, slowly being shaped, ready to be polished into a statue, painful yet necessary. Out of all the breakthroughs, the most significant turning point for me was when Rhonda called me. She said that I wasn't going to make it, I was acting like a victim, I was stunned to hear it so plainly, but it was one thousand percent true. I folded immediately, agreed, and asked for help. She tasked me to find a space where I could be alone to let it all out, to give it to the wind and earth.

I ended up walking 20,000 steps into the desert next to the canal, and boy, did I let it out. I screamed, cussed, cried, kicked the dirt, and flailed about like I was having an exorcism. It certainly felt like one. My eyes were raw, my throat scorched, and my feet blistered. But I was light. Lighter than I had ever felt before. I had never truly let it out until that moment, and it showed. I felt renewed and grateful, and others noticed, too.

After that moment, I pushed through the six-week challenge perfectly with no issues, had no doubt, woke up easily, cooked, worked out, and never struggled again! I'm just kidding; that's not real. Humans are born to flow like the tides, lows and highs, rainy days and sunny days. It's all needed to expand our being; it's simply nature. I continued to do my due diligence daily, journaling my hopes and worries, practicing silence, pushing through workouts, eating right, and participating in class. The homework, activities, and each class taught were nothing short of eye-opening revelations, even when they felt cruel. I learned many things, such as how we're like the buffalo, respecting your enemy, and turning pain into power. I committed to activities like what was on my plate (Instructor Bridget Whitney), writing my eulogy (Instructor Rhonda Sue), and divorcing my past (Instructor Joseph Gause).

One of my favorite lessons was about our cup full of love and divine gifts. Often, we pour ourselves into others until we are empty and dry. All while the other person is asking for more, ungrateful as ever. I used to blame them. "All people do is take from me". Until I realized it was my fault for being so generous. If you leave $20 on a table, someone will take it. That's just human nature. You could give your clothes and bare flesh away, and they'd call you selfish for wanting to keep your bones.

The truth? You are valuable, which is why they come back for more. Don't pour yourself into everyone carelessly; be "selfish." I say selfish because friends and family will call you all sorts of negative projections to bring you back to a point where they benefited from your lack of boundaries. But is it selfish to live your own life? No one else is going to live it for you, so own it. After being empty for so long, discovering or uncovering what elevates your soul or excites you will probably take some time. Maybe you already know; if so, follow that feeling. Let Spirit flow into you, and eventually, your cup will overflow onto those who actually need it most, not just another vampire or fixer-upper. You'll shine and you'll be the light for others without sacrificing your divinity.

Another revelation came during our eulogy exercise. As I was sobbing and stuttering, reading over what I enjoyed, my accomplishments, and my regrets, it clicked in my heart. Something so obvious yet hidden in plain sight: I love myself. Despite the setbacks, the regrets, and all the things I wished I'd done differently, it didn't really matter in the face of death; I'd do it all over again. We waste so much time punishing ourselves based on outdated narratives created by others and society that we forget to appreciate that we are who we are, no one else. We are not here forever; be grateful for the sun and the rain, both are needed for growth.

Setbacks are a part of the journey. You can only see the top of the mountain from the valley, and you can't appreciate the climb without looking back in awe of how far you've come. That's when you decide on a new mountain to climb. It's continuous, cyclical, like everything else in nature. When you feel hopeless, drowning in resentment, guilt, loss of direction, and the pressure of it all, reframe it. Creation and destruction are the same coin; one cannot be without the other. See it both ways, yes, it's falling apart, and it's also coming together. Into something new, something meant for you. Take more moments to honor everything you've survived. You're still here and still rising.

On our days of silence, I felt like I was going insane. "There's the addict," I would say to myself as I was detoxing from the constant distractions, coercing me with their sweet nothings. I lifted the veil of denial on my flaws, seeing the less-than-pleasant sides of being human, and accepted them for what they are. We have them all. Rage, hate, envy, lust, attention seeking, people pleasing, and more. I learned so much about myself and the parts we like to say that we don't experience. If you ask someone if they've manipulated or lied before, they say, "Oh goodness, not me, never". They are full of shit. If you thought the same, then you are also a fool. Own and know your darkness and flaws, lest they be used against you, either by another or yourself.

Finally, it was divorce day, and I was excited and nervous as I fiddled with my dress shirt cuffs on the couch. I had written and compiled evidence on why I should be divorced from my old self. It contained all the formidable work required of me, and more I'd completed on my own over the past six weeks. I was surprised when I saw it all in front of me. A testament to myself and how bad I wanted to leave the past behind, and I was proud. I was ready to face the judge. Once the court was in session, the tune changed drastically.

It was no joking matter. I took a deep breath and laid out all my cards. My past self wasted my time over and over with men who never loved me and abused me. She had funneled thousands of dollars into weed, alcohol, and horrible partners, placing me into a mountain of debt. She hated herself so much for being with a man who was just like her father that she wanted to die. She barely ate until her body atrophied to the point of no return, and we were hospitalized. It almost cost me my own life. I was done; I was tired of repeating it all.

After explaining my reason for this and showcasing my evidence, the defendant's attorney responded, saying they weren't convinced. After pondering and explaining step by step how I knew I wouldn't revert, the judge stopped me, saying he didn't want to hear that, and asked me again, "How do you know you're not going to go back?" I stopped and realized what I was doing. I was overexplaining. But there was no need to do that anymore. I responded, "I just know." My divorce was finalized. Don't let someone else's opinion, perspective, or emotions sway you; let them believe whatever they want. It's not your job to sit and argue with someone else about who you are and what you're doing with your life. Use your energy wisely.

"What is my purpose?" A woodpecker that had been in the back of my brain for years, creating a feverish anxiety that time was slipping through my fingers. I never knew what to do with myself. But during the past six weeks, I finally realized it was right in front of my face. I laughed until I cried. I needed some help seeing it. Words cannot describe the amount of gratitude I feel for those life-altering six weeks, the support of my sisterhood, and all my teachers who poured their time into me, something that can never be returned. So instead of words. I'll show it through my results.

Debra Goodwyn

My Journey to Becoming Unbreakable

What brought me to this group was the fact that I wanted more for myself. For most of my life, I carried a heavy secret that shaped how I saw myself, trusted others, and navigated the world. As a young girl, I was abused. I didn't tell anyone. Not a soul. I buried the pain, locked it deep inside, and wore a mask that smiled, laughed, and lived.

Decades passed, I grew older, but the little girl inside me never stopped whispering, never stopped hurting. I didn't speak about the abuse until I was over 60 years old. I first shared my story with a group of women-sisters in spirit, my Circle of Love family. I will never forget that night. The words Ms. Toni spoke in the group finally opened me up and allowed me to share. As the words left my mouth, my voice trembled, my heart pounded, and my body remembered.

Something happened that I didn't expect: a release. The weight began to lift. I cried-not just tears of pain, but of freedom. For the first time, I didn't feel alone in my truth. I was seen, I was heard, and most of all, I was no longer silenced by shame. That moment was the beginning of healing. That day, the silence broke, and I began healing not just for myself, but for the little girl I used to be. For the woman I am today. I wanted to continue my journey of healing, and that's why I took this course. I signed up for the course thinking it was just another step, another box to check on this long journey of healing. But I didn't know what I was really signing up for, which was myself, my story, my silence, and my emotions.

I opened doors that had been locked for years. They asked us to talk about our feelings. Feelings? I had become a master of not feeling. Of pushing pain to the side; of smiling through storms and saying "I'm fine" while bleeding on the inside. But this course didn't allow me to hide. It asked questions that cracked me open. It held up mirrors I wasn't ready to face. It made space for the little girl I'd silenced, the woman I'd ignored, and the tears I thought I had already cried. I wanted to quit because when you've spent a lifetime keeping the lid on your emotions, peeling it off feels like an explosion.

Then I felt something I hadn't felt in a long time. Relief, freedom, and truth! Saying it out loud took away the power of the pain, the fear, the guilt, and the shame. Piece by piece, layer by layer, tear by tear. I started feeling, and I didn't fall apart. This course didn't just teach me, it touched me. I'll never be the same. Saying goodbye to Debra, this is the one class that I will never forget. We had to write our own eulogy.

At first, I froze. How do you write goodbye to someone who lived inside you for so long? She wasn't just a version of me; she was me. She was the girl who kept the secret. The one who smiles when it hurts. The one who carried shame as if it were her name. I sat there with pen in hand, and tears started falling before the ink ever touched the page.

How do you say goodbye to the girl who kept you alive? The one who protected you by hiding the pain, by shutting down the feelings, by putting on a mask. It's like a funeral and a birth all at once. As I read it aloud, my voice cracked, my hands shook, because letting go of pain sometimes hurts more than holding onto it. Somewhere in goodbye, I found grace. Somewhere in the tears, I found peace. When I laid her to rest, I didn't bury my worth and my wounds. I made space for the Unbreakable Woman I'm becoming. A woman who feels, who speaks, who stands. A woman who no longer lives in the shadow of what happened to her, but who lives in the light of who she's becoming.

To the instructors, the ones who dared to walk with us through our pain, thank you. You didn't just teach a course; you opened a door. A door I didn't know I had the strength to walk through. You created a space where masks could fall, walls crumble, and tears could speak louder than words. In that space, we found courage, truth, and we saw each other. Most of all, we found ourselves.

That eulogy assignment broke me, but it also set me free. The assignment asked us to say goodbye to the pain, to the version of ourselves that had only known survival. In doing that, we gave ourselves permission to live. From the deepest part of my heart, thank you. We are rising, we are becoming, and we will never forget the ones who helped us rise.

Many of us navigate life merely existing rather than truly living, absorbing information without fully grasping its meaning. Growth begins when we reach a point where we genuinely desire to become a changed person. I spent all my time working and with my family. I worked the night shift, so that didn't leave much time for socializing. So, I retired, but that didn't change my life. I was the caregiver for my mother and daughter. I didn't take the time to socialize; that's on me. In July of 2024, I woke up with these words on my mind. Nothing changes if nothing changes! I was ready. That's when my journey to becoming the best version of myself started.

I spent the morning exercising and reading, but I wasn't journaling. I would spend the morning outside in silence. I enjoyed listening to the birds chirping and watching the clouds moving across the sky. It was in those quiet moments that I realized behaviors and emotions from the past. I knew it was God talking to me. Thoughts came to mind, and I knew it was the little girl inside of me who needed to heal. I finally recognized the person who had been there, and I could tell her, "I love you and I got you." That was just the beginning. I knew I had more work to do.

I was following Purpose and Resilience on TikTok. The night Joe spoke of the Unbreakable Woman's page on

Facebook, I immediately joined. I was ready to make a change in my life. I wasn't living, and I wasn't enjoying life. In the group, we had books chosen by Joe for us to read. Each book was a stepping-stone towards our healing. Next was the six-week challenge. I wasn't sure if I could complete the challenge because of the requirements, but it was time to do something for myself and set the doubt aside.

December 2, 2024, was the first day of the challenge. I was up at 4:20 AM. My alarm was set so I could do my video and have it posted by 4:30 AM. I would pray, read, meditate, and journal before the workout. I've acquired a routine for the next six weeks. That day, I decided to delete all the old and start fresh. By the end of the first week of the class, I knew I had made the right decision. My eyes were open to things I hadn't taken the time to process. The discussion on predators and human predators made me face some serious issues.

We must participate in the classes; we can't just sit there and not engage in conversation. I'm not used to sharing my thoughts, so that was a different experience for me. We had to share; I could see myself in every woman who shared their experiences. We had to bring a mirror to class. The second night, I looked at myself in the mirror as everyone spoke, and I asked myself, "Why do you look so angry?" That brought to mind the many times I have been out, and someone would walk past me and say, "Smile." I finally saw the image that others saw. I had to change that. I realized I needed to work on my self-awareness. I needed to move forward and forget things that happened to me in the past. I needed to live and smile.

When asked, "Have you ever compared yourself to someone?" I can honestly say no. I love who I am; I just need to make some changes. I have been so busy doing things for others that I didn't have time to think about comparing myself to anyone else. But I need to set boundaries and goals and be kind to myself. By the second week, I woke up before the alarm went off. I changed the alarm time to 4:00 AM. I was starting to develop the skill of discipline. I'm reading, journaling, and taking the time to think about what I'm reading.

Every morning, I would write a scripture, and it started to make sense. I have come to realize that many mistakes and poor decisions will be made in life. Doors open that we should not walk through, doors open that we should have gone through, but we were afraid. Life is a journey that I am constantly learning from daily. If I am not learning, I am not living. I was also at a point where I no longer wanted to be angry. I have looked at the mistakes and choices I've made, and I am at peace with them. I no longer want to dwell on the past; I want to remove the mask and put it all behind me. I tell myself, "I am enough because God created me." "I am unique." "I am a one-of-a-kind person, and no one can be like me." "I am love and I have a heart of gold.' "I am amazing."

I can't let others' betrayals cause me to doubt myself. I own my future, not the wounds of my past. I want to share a scripture that I wrote one morning. Ephesians 3:20 "Now to him who can do immeasurably more than all we ask or imagine, according to his power at work within us." As I read those words, I realized that I have the power within me, with the help of the Holy Spirit. I can achieve peace from the past and move on with the Holy Spirit inside of me. Thank you, God!

I have not wasted time, but I have grown and learned. Together, we have healed that little girl inside of us. This course covered topics such as people-pleasing, developing discipline, emotional healing, and self-awareness. People Pleasing and Manipulation. I was a people pleaser. As far back as I can remember, I have always done things to please others in friendships, relationships, and even at work. It brings to mind a relationship I was in a couple of years ago. When I discussed his behavior with a gentleman, he immediately switched the topic, which made me feel like it was my fault, that I was wrong, and that I was causing issues in the relationship. I had a gut feeling that something was wrong, and it was. He was married.

Ladies, when you have a gut feeling about someone, please pay attention to those feelings. Don't let anyone make you feel that your feelings are not valid. I will never forget the way I felt when I found out. When you don't have love, you look for it, not realizing it's inside you. You fall for their words because you have never heard them before. Just love yourself and say those words to yourself. Then you won't fall for them without question when someone tells you. People-pleasing can be very emotional and lead to low self-esteem and manipulation. I have learned to say no, set boundaries, and no longer put others before myself. I will no longer be a people pleaser.

Discipline

Discipline is about showing up and requires accountability. It creates consistency in your life and builds endurance. Discipline starts with a decision: "I want better for myself." "This healing journey is one that I won't stop.". On those days when I felt like giving up, I get myself in the mirror and say "bitch, not today". You have to keep moving. I know there may be setbacks, forgive yourself, and start over. Discipline is also about consistency and accountability. Since the course ended, I have continued with my morning routine. I get up every morning and spend time in quiet reflection, prayer, and meditation. I don't journal every morning, but I need to make sure I do. I continue to eat healthy. I only exercise for forty-five minutes four times a week because of a fall injury. I know I have to keep showing up for myself and my health.

Awareness

A seed story was one of my favorite classes in the course. From darkness to light, a journey of growth, pain, and greatness is just what this course is about. When you hear and understand that your pain isn't wasted but waiting for its moment, you know! You realize that all the pain you experience is something that you can learn from. The darkness is where the seed finds its roots. It digs deeper not because it's being punished, but because it's being prepared.

I'm planting a garden this year, which makes sense. You're planting that seed in the soil (darkness). The darkness trains you for the light. My seedlings are reaching for the light, have roots, and are now ready to be transplanted. When you take the time to sit in silence and go back to those experiences that made you feel less than and unloved, you can learn something about yourself. You grow and are now ready to transplant yourself into a new life.

Forgive yourself and move on.

I forgave myself the night I said goodbye to the old Debra. I realized that no one could hurt you more than you hurt yourself. You can't place your happiness in the hands of someone else. Your happiness comes from within. I am aware and pay more attention to the things happening around me, inside me, and spoken words. I realize that I can't be everything to everybody. I make time for things that are important to me, and to me, that means growth.

December 31, 2024

Today is the last day of 2024. It's been a year of many ups and downs, bumps and bruises. As the song says, "bruised but not broken." I have made some unwise choices, but I've survived them and moved on. I have peace now and am working towards new goals for 2025. Time is moving, I have to start living life and enjoying whatever time I have left on this earth. I have healed from all my past relationships. I'm not calling them mistakes because I learned from each of them.

I entered the new year with peace, a peace that cannot be taken away from me by others. At the end of this course, I learned that at a certain point in life, you have to take responsibility for the decisions you make. You can't blame others for the things you decided to do, even if they caused you pain. Take responsibility and move on. Don't stay stuck on them. Learn from them, reflect on them. What did you learn?

Every decision you make offers something to learn. Look at who you are, the person you are becoming. Sometimes, we become stuck and remain in that place, unsure of which direction to take. Then someone comes into your life and changes how you look and think about life. That is what this course did for me. You go from just living daily to becoming more aware of your day-to-day experiences.

Remember, everything in life is a process in motion. Start building a foundation for a fulfilling life. Live in the present, don't go back. Embrace challenges as opportunities for growth and cultivate a growth mindset. To grow, you must forgive others and, most importantly, yourself. Get rid of your hatred, and you will have the desired peace. I have closed this journal in the past. I now have a new journal with new adventures. I want to thank each of the women who were on this journey with me. Each one taught me something different. The discipline Nicole is still teaching is so impressive. The journey continues!

I also want to thank the instructors of this course. Each one is truly a gem: Joseph Gause, Bridget Whitney, Kauri Mowell, Tameika Marrow, and Robin Sue. Thank you for sharing your wisdom, stories, and skills with us. Your willingness to pour into others and teach from experience means more than you know. Each of you made learning feel real, inspiring, and empowering. Thank you for showing up with grace and strength. Keep shining and being amazing.

Astride Candice

The Awakening of the Unbreakable: The Woman That Was Always Me!

When I signed up for the six-week Unbreakable Woman course on self-discipline, I didn't go in feeling strong. I went in desperate. I was tired of living life in cycles, starting and stopping, doubting myself, and talking myself out of everything I wanted. I knew I needed change, but I was terrified of what that actually meant. Change isn't just about building better habits; it's about letting go of who you were pretending to be.

I had gotten really comfortable hiding behind fear, self-doubt, and all the lies I told myself: "I'm not capable," "I'm not as confident as her," "I'll probably fail anyway." The course wasn't magic; it didn't give me some perfect, polished version of myself. What it did was force me to meet myself, the real me, the one underneath the layers of low self-esteem, people-pleasing, and constant self-doubt. I had to face the version of me that didn't believe she was enough.

I didn't think she had what it took to show up every day and keep a promise to herself. I won't lie; it was messy. There were days I wanted to quit. I'd be journaling or pushing through a new routine, and suddenly, I'd hear that old voice in my head: "You're not good at this, you'll never finish anything." But I kept going. Not because I felt like it every day,

108

but because I had finally decided that I was worth the effort. The old me was scared and afraid, but the new me kept showing up. She made it this far.

During the course, I realized healing and discipline weren't about becoming someone else but about coming back to myself, the unbreakable me. One of the biggest turning points for me during the course was when we had to do the mirror exercise. I had just finished reading Sovereign, and something in me cracked open. That book made me realize how disconnected I was from myself. I'd been moving through life, surviving, managing, fixing, but I wasn't checking in with myself, not really. I never paused to ask, "How am I really doing?" or "What do I need?" Then came that mirror exercise, looking into my own eyes and talking to the woman I'd been avoiding for years.

At first, I stood there frozen, feeling silly. Then I started speaking, and something came out of me that I didn't even know I had been holding. I screamed, I cried, I let it all pour out. I told myself how sorry I was for not protecting my own heart, for putting everyone else first while silently drowning. For letting fear, pride, insecurity, and the wounds from my past, especially the scars left by domestic abuse, keep me small.

That moment shattered me and freed me at the same time. I saw myself for who I was, not just the broken pieces, but the fighter underneath. I saw the woman who made it through so much and still had the courage to want more. I realized I hadn't let myself down because I was weak; I let myself down because I was scared, tired, and didn't know how to be there for myself. Now I do. That mirror didn't just reflect my face; it reflected the truth.

I want every woman reading this to know you are allowed to break down, you are allowed to feel all of it. You are allowed to scream and cry and grieve the parts of yourself you had to let go of. What matters is that you come back for you. That you stop waiting for someone else to validate your pain, and instead hold space for it yourself. You are not weak for feeling lost. You are powerful for being willing to find your way back.

Another impactful lesson was when we were asked during the course, "What's on your plate?" Simple question, right? It hit me like a wave. I sat there, pen in hand, and for the first time, I got honest about what I'd been carrying, not just in my schedule, but in my spirit. I realized my plate wasn't full of to-do lists or busy routines; it was full of emotional weight I hadn't named out loud. I was carrying trauma from abuse, heavy and silent. I was carrying envy from my divorce, watching someone move on while I was still picking up pieces that left me broken and ashamed. I carried the burden of trying to be perfect, always thinking I had to earn love or prove my worth. The scariest part? I was so used to carrying it all that I thought it was normal.

That day, something shifted. I saw my old plate as overloaded, unbalanced, and not serving the woman I was becoming. I decided to build a new plate, one that reflected the life I wanted, not just the pain I survived. Now, my plate looks different. It holds habits that feed my soul when asked, "What is your worth? How do you value yourself?" I wrote to myself. I value myself by how I show up for myself every day, crafting and working on self-mastery, aka self-discipline, and perfecting the craft of feeding my mind with information that will benefit my future. I've learned that working out stimulates my body and mind.

I've realized that following a schedule or routine sets the tone for the day. Being self-aware and fixing the mistakes that will come along the way. Ultimately, I will put myself first by any means necessary. I will choose to surround myself with people who will feed my mind, mentors and friends who will help me grow. Even after the plate challenge, the course didn't magically become easier for me; it got harder. Life didn't pause just because I was healing. I got sick twice, one of those times, I was battling bronchitis, and the cough stuck around like it had something to prove. I was exhausted. My body was worn out, and my mind wasn't far behind. There were mornings I woke up and thought, "How much more can I take?" I kept showing up. Not because I felt good or strong, but because I was determined.

I was done living as the version of myself that made excuses, that put everyone else before her well-being, that believed pain was just a permanent part of life. I knew that old self wasn't serving me anymore. She helped me survive, but wasn't going to help me grow. So, I pushed, sometimes too hard. I pushed past my comfort zone; I pushed through the ache in my chest. I pushed through the fog in my head, the voice that said, "Just rest, just quit, you've done enough." Deep down, I hadn't. Not yet. I knew what I was fighting for. This wasn't just a course. It was a reckoning, a breakdown of every version of myself I had created to stay safe, small, and unnoticed. I was ripping off layers of fear, pride, resentment, and habits that made me feel in control, but kept me stuck.

Yes, I paid for it physically; I felt the toll on my body. I also felt something else start to grow, resilience. Not the loud, showy kind. The quiet kind, the kind that whispers, "Keep going, you're doing the work now. You're almost free." The moment I knew I was finally free wasn't loud. It didn't come with a big celebration or some grand achievement; it was quiet and peaceful. I just stopped caring what people thought of me. Honestly, I stopped shrinking myself to fit into someone else's version of what a "good woman" should be. I stopped carrying the weight of people-pleasing as if it were some badge of honor. I realized I was on a quest to build the best version of me, not for them, but for me.

Honestly, that changed everything. For years, I wore shame like a second skin. The shame of being divorced and the shame of surviving domestic abuse. I carried it in my silence, in the way I didn't correct people when they misunderstood my story, in the way I'd smile and keep things surface-level to avoid judgment. As a South African woman, raised with cultural expectations of endurance, keeping things behind closed doors, and appearing strong no matter what, I thought keeping quiet was strength. I thought surviving quietly was enough, but it wasn't.

That shame robbed me of my voice. It robbed me of the joy I should have felt in finally leaving what was breaking me. I thought I was broken because my marriage failed, because I had been hurt by someone who was supposed to protect me. The truth is, I wasn't broken, I was brave. I chose myself, even when it cost me everything, I thought I was supposed to be. Now, putting my truth out into the world, my real, raw, messy truth, is what's setting me free. Every time I speak it, the shame loses power. Every time I own it, I step more fully into my freedom. I'm no longer hiding behind what happened to me. I'm leading with what I've become because of it.

To any woman carrying shame that doesn't belong to her, please know that your freedom is on the other side of owning your truth. Say it out loud, not for validation, but for liberation. You are not your past. You are who you decide to become now. Implementing the life lessons from the course felt like trying to walk on new legs, unsteady, unsure, but determined. One of the most unexpected challenges came when I silenced myself on social media. That was one of the requirements that I thought was not going to be hard for me.

At first, it felt like freedom. No more pretending, no more performing, no more trying to post a version of me that wasn't always true. Then came the stillness, and with it, the loneliness. The quiet gave my mind space to breathe, but it also allowed my old thoughts to sneak back in. Thoughts like, "Maybe you're not really free," or "Who are you without their likes, and their validation?" That's when I had to confront the truth: just because my marriage was over, just because I walked away from what was hurting me, didn't mean the damage was gone.

The mind that had been manipulated, belittled, and broken still whispered doubts. I was no longer in a cage, but sometimes I felt trapped in my head. So, I kept working every day, and I showed up to build trust with the unbreakable version of myself. The woman I knew was in there, even if I could only see her in glimpses. I talked to her in the mirror. I reminded her of her strength. I gave her grace on the days she wanted to disappear.

Most importantly, I committed to her. To me, because I knew that my story, every scar, every silence, every scream I swallowed, was not just mine to carry. It was mine to share. I believe with my whole heart that I went through this for a reason: to help another woman feel seen. If I could touch just one life with my truth, if one woman could read my words and feel less alone, it's all worth it: the silence, the tears, and the struggle. Every moment of it, healing is hard. Living with purpose is difficult, but pretending was harder. I've made peace with my pain, not by erasing it, but by letting it fuel my calling.

To the woman reading this who's still unsure if her voice matters, it does. Your story can free someone else. First, let it free you. While implementing new habits, a new life came with the "You Owe it To Yourself" class, where we had to face ourselves and divorce the old version of us that no longer served our future. I won't lie; I was scared. Deep down, I knew this was the turning point; this wasn't just another lesson. It was a declaration that I was no longer available for the patterns, mindsets, and fears that had held me hostage for years.

I remember walking into that session with my heart pounding, yet I felt oddly prepared. A strange calm settled over me, not because I had it all figured out, but because something bigger than me was guiding the moment. That's when I remembered the vision board I had made months ago, before I knew I would take this course. It had been sitting in my kitchen the whole time, quietly watching me go through my days. I hadn't even looked at it recently, but that night, I did.

It hit me; everything this course was asking of me, I had already asked of myself. Right there on my vision board were the words I now live by, "focus on yourself, care for your body, and care for your mind. Stay away from toxic people; unfollow them on social media. Talk to the people who stayed through your worst and are still there. Romanticize every moment of your life. "Love yourself." I had written my own permission slip months before I had the courage to live it. That board was a quiet prayer I had whispered to the woman I hoped to become.

When it came time to plead my case, to let go of my old self and fight for the unbreakable woman I was becoming, I realized I'd already begun the process. I had already cut ties with what was toxic. I had already started showing up for myself in small but powerful ways. I had already begun manifesting the life I was now claiming. That night, I didn't just let go of my old self; I honored her. I thanked her for surviving, for keeping me going, even when she was broken, but I told her it was time. Time to make space for the woman

I had been too scared to be. The one who lives on purpose. The one who loves herself without apology. The one who chooses herself, not because she's selfish, but because she finally believes she's worth it.

After we divorced our old selves, the next challenge was something that felt simple on the surface, but it cracked something open in me. We were asked to go on a solo date. Just me, by myself, taking myself out to eat. It may sound small, but to me, it was monumental. I had never done the theatre before. It was the kind of thing I used to avoid, too exposed, too vulnerable, too "what will people think?" I was living out a new life now, I had let go of who I was and stepped into the woman I was becoming.

I got ready that day, and I went to try on new clothes, something I hadn't done in a long time with any real joy. I was so deep into the work of the course, so focused on healing and becoming, that I didn't even realize how much weight I had lost, not just physically, but emotionally and spiritually, too. I grabbed a medium dress and a medium sweater just to see, and they fit. I stood in that dressing room, staring at myself in the mirror, stunned. That reflection was someone I hadn't met yet, strong, softer in some places, glowing in others. And for the first time in a long time, I smiled at her. I spritzed on a new, feminine, and bold perfume and got myself ready like I was going somewhere important, because I was. I was going out to celebrate myself.

At first, sitting in that restaurant alone felt awkward. I kept looking around, wondering if people noticed, wondering if I looked out of place. Then, I called my unbreakable sister Nicole. Just hearing her voice reminded me I wasn't alone. We're never alone when we've done the work that builds sisterhood and self-trust. Her words grounded me. I looked around the restaurant again, but this time, with my head held higher.

Then something unexpected happened. I started to enjoy myself. I tasted the food, sipped slowly, and smiled. I caught a glimpse of myself in the reflection of the glass and saw a woman who wasn't hiding anymore. I saw a proud woman. I even caught a few looks, and for once, I didn't shrink under them. I let myself feel seen, not for approval but as a celebration of how far I'd come. That solo date wasn't just a meal; it was another declaration. I was no longer waiting for someone to make me feel beautiful, special, or worthy. I was living for myself now, fully, proudly, and confidently.

To every woman who's afraid to be seen, who doesn't recognize herself in the mirror yet, please hear me when I say, "Keep going." One day, you'll wear a dress, take yourself out, and realize you are becoming the woman you've always deserved to be.

Aderemi Holloway

From Fragments to Flames

I didn't wake up one day magically ready to change my life. Some lightning bolt of motivation didn't strike me. There was no perfect morning routine, vision board epiphany, or viral quote that suddenly made it all click. If I'm being honest, I didn't even believe I could change, not really. I was surviving. Going through the motions. Telling myself the same lies I'd gotten comfortable living with, "I'll start tomorrow," "I just need to get through this week," "Once things calm down, then I'll focus on me." You know the script.

Eventually, I reached a point where the weight of staying the same felt heavier than the fear of taking action. That's when I found myself signing up for the Unbreakable Woman Challenge. I wasn't sure I could finish, and what followed wasn't pretty, it wasn't perfect, and it definitely wasn't linear, but it was real. This isn't a story about becoming flawless. It's not a guide to "finding balance" or "hacking your mindset." It's a story about what happens when you finally stop waiting, when you stop negotiating with your excuses, when you meet the version of yourself you've been avoiding and decide to fight for her instead of against her.

I didn't know it then, but those first shaky steps were leading me somewhere I never thought I'd reach. To a place where discipline became self-love and discomfort became freedom. I realized no one was coming to save me, because I didn't need saving. I just needed to remember who I was before life convinced me to shrink. I'm sharing with you how I did that, one choice, one uncomfortable step at a time. I didn't start this journey unbreakable, but I damn sure ended it knowing I could become.

No Longer Negotiable

I didn't realize the weight I was carrying until I set it down. When I started the Unbreakable Woman Challenge, I thought I was signing up for discipline and routines, maybe a little motivation to get my life together. What I didn't expect was the mirror it would hold up to me. The kind you can't look away from, no matter how uncomfortable the reflection gets. This wasn't just a program; it was a reckoning. From day one, I was almost kicked out. "You were supposed to be kicked out on day two, but God had other plans for me."

"Chosen," That's what she said we were, that I was. At first, I didn't know how to receive that. I wanted to believe it, but it felt like a title meant for someone else. Someone stronger, someone more consistent, and someone who didn't have a habit of breaking promises to herself. Chosen or not, the challenge had begun, and it hit me fast just how much I'd been negotiating with my potential. The first few days were brutal in the most ordinary ways. Getting out of bed felt like a war. My body ached like it was punishing me for even daring to move. Every excuse I'd ever used showed up, louder than ever. Yet, I kept going, I took walks with my dad in those first couple of days, dragging my feet through every step.

I started to notice how much time I wasted scrolling since setting down social media. How my mind wandered the second I tried to be present. Paying attention to what I was eating felt like learning a foreign language. I was standing in my kitchen, staring at food like it had betrayed me. "So... I can't just eat whatever's easy and pretend it counts?" I caught myself slipping into old patterns: people-pleasing, looking for validation, feeling invisible over stupid things like not being offered breakfast at work, and I hated how much it mattered to me, but this week wasn't just about noticing my patterns. It was about confronting them. That's when I wrote something I didn't realize would stay with me.

I Am Not a Fighter, But a Warrior (Full passage taken directly from Journal)

I kept ruminating after class because something felt stuck. I felt like I was on the edge of something, and it finally clicked. The instructor asked a question, and what I realized was that the betrayal of self in class was the fact that I felt that

I betrayed the little girl in me. At the time, I didn't have the proper words to articulate this until last night, when the puzzle pieces finally clicked. I let others take my power away from me, or I gave them power over me. Yes, I couldn't control what happened to me as a child, but the fact that I let these habits continue as an adult is my fault. It gets to be my fault, and by virtue of my taking on this "blame," I have the chance to fix it. It is my responsibility.

Truth be told, it didn't feel extremely daunting, taking this on. However, for the first time in a long time, I feel as if I'm not just fooling myself into some untruthful and unearned form of positivity; I think I can sort of see the way out. As a child, I wrote this poem titled "I am not A Fighter," but a warrior. I think it was written as a response to what my dad and I were conversing about. He labeled me a fighter; for some reason, that didn't entirely resonate with me. I couldn't put my finger on why. So, I looked up the definition of a fighter, which is defined as "a person or animal that fights, especially as a soldier or a boxer." Then I found warrior, "a brave or experienced fighter." For some reason, I felt drawn to that word. Warrior. Maybe this was a more accurate depiction of me, or who I hoped to become.

I thought a fighter was someone who just pushed endlessly, bloody, bruised, gnashing their teeth against life, never knowing when to stop or how to rise above survival mode. I didn't want that; I didn't want to fight just to exist. I wanted to reach farther, burn hotter, live deeper. Instead of chasing life, I let the comfort of fear cage me. I bought into the safe path, I betrayed that little voice inside that told me, "You're meant for more." What I didn't understand back then was that you must be a fighter before you can become a warrior. You must get knocked down, you must bleed, you must get back up, over and over, until resilience becomes part of your DNA. That's how you become unbreakable.

When I finished writing that, I sat there for a long time staring up at my ceiling. Looking back, I didn't realize how important those words would become. At the time, it felt like I was just venting, trying to make sense of why life always felt like a fight I wasn't winning. Now, I was beginning to understand this wasn't about proving anything to anyone else. I wasn't losing because I was weak. I was avoiding the necessary battle. I thought I could think my way into transformation. If I just visualized the life I wanted hard enough, I wouldn't have to bleed for it. I was wrong. You don't get to become without being broken down first. You don't get to call yourself a warrior if you've never stood back up after falling, again, and again, and again.

This week taught me that discipline isn't about forcing perfection; it's about refusing to abandon yourself when things get uncomfortable, inconvenient, or lonely. This transformation was about burning away every lie I'd told myself about who I was and what I could endure. This journey was and still is about realizing that no one's coming to save you from your own patterns. That's a good thing because it means you don't need to be saved; you need to decide that comfort is no longer your god.

I didn't want complacency, I didn't want survival, I wanted to soar higher, reach farther, burn brighter than I ever thought possible. I wanted to be unbreakable, but wanting it and becoming it? That's where the real war begins. That was the first week I stopped trying. It was the week I picked up my sword. Welcome to Week 1.

Patterns, Pitfalls, and Picking Up the Pieces

Week two didn't come with a surge of motivation. It came with silence, which forces you to listen to the thoughts you usually drown out. That's when I realized the real battle wasn't with the workouts, the early mornings, or food. It was with my own patterns. I caught myself scrolling again, news articles, mind you, when I had never been one to read the news before. I never realized that even something as simple and mind-numbing as scrolling could be used as a tool to self-soothe. I fantasized about skipping my workout because "technically, I deserved rest."

I caught myself getting petty over not being invited to some dumb office breakfast like I was 12 years old on the playground watching everyone else get picked first. It was like watching my old self in real-time, trying to pull me back into comfort. Honestly, I almost let her, but something was different this time. I wasn't giving in, I was watching. I was aware. Awareness is where change starts. Then, out of nowhere, a lyric popped into my head: "Ruthlessness is Mercy Upon Ourselves." When I first heard it, I brushed it off as poetic dramatics. Lyrics that hit hard in the context of a song. I love musicals, but nothing more. Now? Now, it felt personal. I looked up the definition of ruthless, which means having or showing no compassion or pity for others.

In the song, Poseidon tells Odysseus that if he'd been ruthless and killed Poseidon's son, he would've spared himself the wrath that followed. Mercy, in that moment, had a price. Suddenly, it clicked. Ruthlessness is mercy upon us. If you show mercy to your enemies, you give them space to regroup, come back stronger, and take you down. What if you are your greatest enemy? I know how I think. I know my fears, my triggers, my weaknesses. I know exactly which levers to pull to make myself retreat. So, how do you fight an enemy who knows you that well? You don't negotiate. You don't show pity for the patterns that are trying to kill your potential. You get ruthless. Not cruel, not self-hating, but uncompromising with anything that tries to drag you back into who you used to be.

That realization didn't fix everything overnight, but it gave me a new weapon. By the end of the week, I had decided. I wasn't going to keep dipping my toe into this commitment. I wasn't going to wait for motivation to magically carry me through. I was going all in. The food, the mindset, the discipline, I was done playing nice with my excuses. I wasn't interested in seeing how long I could "try." I wanted to see how far I could go if I stopped giving myself an out. It wasn't a loud moment, no dramatic music. Just me, sitting in my room, tired of my own negotiations. That's when I realized, sometimes, the most powerful thing you can say to yourself is simple: "We're doing this, no matter what." Once I said it, I meant it. That was the week I stopped asking for permission from others and myself. It was the week I chose to be ruthless, because I finally understood that it was the kindest thing I could do.

The Edge of Old Habits

There's a moment in every journey where the excitement wears off, and all you're left with is you, your habits, and the quiet question: "Are you really about this, or were you just chasing a feeling?" Week three was that moment for me. The initial spark, the adrenaline of "I'm changing my life," had burned out. What remained was the uncomfortable truth that discipline wasn't exciting. It was repetitive, it was boring, it was showing up when the only person who'd know if you quit was you. I was dangerously close to quitting. Not in a dramatic, throw-in-the-towel kind of way, but in the subtle, familiar way I'd always done before. I'd let things slide, telling myself I'd "get back on track tomorrow," watching my commitment dissolve before I could even admit I was slipping. This time, I didn't let myself fall all the way back.

I was teetering on the edge of old habits, but I caught myself. I realized that every excuse I was making wasn't new. I heard them all before, I lost to them before, but I didn't have to lose this time. That awareness, that pause before giving in, that was growth. It didn't feel like a victory at the time. It felt like dragging myself through mud, questioning why I even started. When I look back, I see it clearly. That was the week I learned discipline isn't a feeling. It's a decision you make every single day, whether you feel like it or not.

I wasn't perfect, and I didn't hit every goal, but I didn't quit. Sometimes, not quitting is the most powerful thing you can do. By the end of the week, I wasn't proud of my performance, but I was proud of one thing: I didn't disappear on myself. I spent years ghosting my potential; the second things got uncomfortable, but this time, I stayed. Bruised ego, messy execution, and all, I stayed in the fight, and that's when

I realized something no one tells you about growth. It doesn't always appear to be progress. Sometimes, it seems like refusing to backslide. Sometimes, it looks like standing still when every part of you wants to run. Week three wasn't pretty, but it was pivotal. I proved to myself that I was done being the kind of person who only shows up when it's easy. I was becoming the kind of woman who shows up regardless.

The Death of "Old Me"

There's something about late December that makes everyone suddenly reflective. New Year's resolutions. Fresh starts. The whole "new year, new me" fantasy. This year was different; I wasn't waiting for January 1st to flip some imaginary switch. I was already in the fire, and I've been burning away the old me for weeks. Still, there was something gratifying about knowing I started this journey before the rest of the world began its annual cycle of empty promises. While everyone else was planning to change, I was already in the trenches doing it. But starting early didn't make me immune to my old patterns. If anything, it exposed them.

I realized how many lies I'd gotten comfortable telling myself, how often I'd confused "intentions" with action. How easy it was to romanticize change but avoid the actual work. The truth hit hard: Resolutions don't change you; choices do. I already made up my mind weeks ago, but that choice came with a cost I wasn't prepared for. I wasn't ready for the quiet, creeping grief of letting go of who I used to be. No one talks about that part, the mourning. I thought becoming a better version of myself would feel empowering, and sometimes it did. But other times, it felt like I was killing off parts of me I'd relied on for years. The excuses that kept me comfortable.

The habits that numbed the discomfort. The identity I'd built around being "the one who never follows through." Letting go of that version of me felt like losing an old friend, a toxic friend, sure, but one that had been there through everything. I remember sitting in my room one night, staring at the clutter I was supposed to be cleaning, feeling this weird mix of exhaustion and fear. Who was I without my procrastination? Without my self-sabotage? Without my excuses? That's when it hit me; I wasn't just "improving," I was burying the version of myself that kept me small. Funerals, no matter how necessary, are never fun.

I felt something emerge somewhere between that grief and the growing pains: A quiet pride, because every day I chose discipline over comfort, I was proving to myself that I didn't need to be saved. I didn't need a new year, a fresh start, or permission from anyone. I just needed to keep showing up. By the time December 31st rolled around, I didn't feel the urge to make resolutions. I didn't need to "start over." I was already becoming. When I looked ahead, I realized I wasn't afraid of leaving the old me behind anymore. I was ready to light the match.

Becoming the Woman Who Follows Through

There's a strange moment when you realize, "I'm not the same person who started this." It doesn't come with fireworks or some big announcement. Just a quiet awareness that the things you used to avoid you're handling now. The promises you used to break, you're keeping. That was week five for me. I found myself doing things automatically that used to feel impossible. Waking up early wasn't a debate; it was just what I did. Working out wasn't a punishment; it was a commitment, and I wasn't negotiating with myself every five minutes anymore.

I couldn't believe how far I'd come in such a surprisingly short time. I knew I still had a long road ahead, growth doesn't have a finish line, but I'd gone from doubting if I could change at all, to showing myself that I could do anything I truly committed to. When I looked in the mirror for the first time in a long time, I felt a flicker of pride. Not because I was perfect, not because I had it all figured out, but because I was becoming a woman who followed through. The kind of woman who did what she said she'd do, even when no one was watching. Even when it wasn't convenient.

Even when the old me whispered, "It's okay to skip just this once." I wasn't chasing motivation anymore. I was building momentum. With that momentum came something I hadn't expected: trust. I finally trusted myself to handle hard things. To stay consistent. To not abandon my goals, the second life threw a curveball. That trust was worth more than my external validation. It was quiet, it was steady, and it was mine. By the end of the week, I realized something even bigger: This wasn't about a 6-week challenge anymore. It was about rewriting the way I showed up for myself, permanently. I wasn't interested in being the girl who started strong but faded out. I was determined to be the woman who finishes and then keeps going. Once you prove to yourself that you can follow through, you stop asking, "Can I do this?" You start asking: "What else am I capable of?"

Quiet Victories and Endless Possibilities

Graduation day didn't feel how I expected. There was no dramatic transformation, sudden feeling of "I've made it." No finish line energy. I logged off the Zoom call, closed my laptop, and realized my alarm would still ring at 2 AM tomorrow. That's when it hit me: the real victory wasn't in finishing the program. It was in who I'd become along the way. There was no applause when I laced up my shoes the next morning. No one is cheering because I chose discipline over comfort, again. But I didn't need the noise. I finally understood that the quiet victories are the ones that matter most.

Every time I showed up, no one was watching. I kept every promise to myself when quitting would've been easier. Every small, consistent choice that no one else would ever notice, that's where I won. I used to think success would feel loud. Now I know, it feels steady, it feels like trusting yourself to keep going, long after the motivation fades. Graduation wasn't a finish line. It was a threshold. I wasn't done, I was just getting started, and for the first time, I wasn't overwhelmed by how far I still had to go.

I was excited because now I knew I could rely on myself. The possibilities ahead didn't feel intimidating anymore. They felt endless. I wasn't asking for permission. I wasn't waiting for the "right time." I wasn't wondering if I could stay consistent. I'd already proven I could. The spark I was searching for at the beginning of this journey? It didn't come from the program. It didn't come from anyone else; it came from me. From every moment, I chose to rise when it would've been easier to stay the same. Now, the flame is mine.

The Flame is Mine Now

It was never about a program. Sure, the Unbreakable Woman Challenge gave me the tools. It gave me structure, accountability, and a reason to start. It gave me the framework.

But the real work? The real transformation? That was always between me and the woman in the mirror. No one was coming to save me, no one could force me to wake up at 2 AM, and no one could make me keep a promise when it was easier to break it. It was always going to be me vs. me. I met her somewhere between the early mornings, the aching muscles, the quiet realizations, and the days I wanted to quit but didn't.

The woman I'd been avoiding my whole life was not the perfect version I used to fantasize about. Not some flawless, fearless ideal. But a woman who was becoming steady, disciplined, and aware. A woman who didn't need motivation because she'd built something stronger, self-respect. I'm still getting to know her. Every day, I learn a little more about what she's capable of. Every day, I choose to stand beside her, even when it's hard, especially when it's hard. That's what being unbreakable really means.

It's not about never falling. It's about refusing to abandon yourself when you do. It's showing up when no one's watching. It's keeping the promises that only you will know if you kept. It's understanding that strength isn't something you're given, it's something you build, quietly, every day. I started this journey hoping for a spark, some burst of motivation to finally light the fire under me. What I found was something better. I found proof that I could trust myself, I found discipline where there used to be doubt, and I found a flame that doesn't flicker every time life gets hard. Now, I know the truth. There's no going back to who I was, and I wouldn't want to. The spark survived. The flame is mine now.

Arletta F. Saafir

Becoming Unbreakable

I've been walking this healing and evolutionary path ever since I stepped away from organized patriarchal religion back in 2004. Since then, I've picked up and worked through all kinds of tools to break free from emotional and energetic blockages, to heal trauma, low self-esteem, and the patterns that had me stuck, especially when it came to creating and manifesting the life I truly desired. For the past three years, I've been deep in a process called Illuminations, it's real inner work that neutralizes trauma, rewires thought patterns, and even helps reprogram the brain and nervous system on an epigenetic level. I had already transformed a lot, but I knew what was missing: discipline. I wasn't showing up for myself consistently. That was my next frontier.

So, when I heard Purpose and Resilience on Priscella the Queenmaker's High Power podcast talking about the Unbreakable Woman Challenge, I didn't hesitate. I immediately jumped on Facebook to see if there was still a chance to join. I requested access, got accepted, and started connecting with the women in the group and the Book Club that was already in motion. From that very first interaction, I knew these women were special. They were laser-focused, determined, and willing to do the real work to change their lives. I thought, these are my people, I want to be around. Purpose? Straight shooter. No fluff. No sugarcoating. Completely unapologetic. Exactly what I needed.

Of course, my guard was up; why would a man offer a free 6-week challenge for women? What's the catch? Turns out, the only catch was showing up. Purpose wasn't playing games. He wasn't building followers; he was building a powerful tribe of serious, disciplined, unshakeable women. I've stepped out on faith plenty of times in my journey, and I was willing to do it again, unless this Challenge turned out to be some BS. Spoiler: and it wasn't. I was nervous but excited. I'd done the 5 AM Club and even upgraded to my own 4 AM Club, so waking up at 4:30 AM didn't scare me, but the level of accountability? That was next level. Clean eating, tracking every meal, walking 5K steps minimum every day? Let's go. I was already taking decent care of myself, but this was about taking it up a notch and locking in the discipline I'd been craving. Note to anyone thinking about doing this Challenge: don't do what I did. READ THE MANUAL!

I didn't fully realize I was signing up for five nights a week of self-improvement classes from 8 PM to 10 PM (and usually closer to 11 PM). I signed up right in the middle of the holiday season, prime time for work events, galas, and endless evening commitments. What was I thinking? I ended up canceling almost everything. I only attended the two events I absolutely couldn't miss. That's how powerful the course was; I didn't want to miss one single class.

Deep Dive: The Real Work

The Unbreakable Woman Challenge is a mental, emotional, and physical boot camp. No sugarcoating and no hiding; you will meet yourself. You will confront your patterns, your victim stories, and your excuses face-to-face. It shook me, it cracked me open, it exposed all the places where I was holding back, and honestly? I loved it. That's what I signed up for. There's a lot of psychology baked into the way Purpose runs this Challenge. Yes, there were mind games, subtle power plays, and psychological pressure, and that's exactly what makes the transformation stick. It's a system designed to break you out of yourself.

What I appreciated most is that the Challenge was created by a man but delivered by a dynamic team of powerful women. Purpose brought structure, accountability, and masculine discipline, which, "let's be real, some of us need to balance out our softness." He didn't coddle us; he didn't let us off the hook, and I thrived in that space. Funny enough, after the Challenge, I revisited the original podcast where I first heard about Purpose. The comments were full of people asking, "What can a man possibly teach women about self-improvement?" Turns out, a man can teach a woman a whole lot. Transformation isn't gendered; truth is truth.

One of the hardest parts for me was six weeks with no social media. I thought, no problem, I can stay off Instagram and Facebook. What I didn't realize was how much I consumed YouTube, geopolitics, finance, ancient African history, Joe Dispenza, all of it. I didn't realize YouTube was my crutch. When I cut it off, I went through real withdrawal. But the beauty of that detox? I started devouring audiobooks again, diving into Goddess worship origins, the Divine Feminine in Christianity, and all of that became part of my healing in ways I didn't expect. The biggest gift was silence. I rediscovered the joy and wisdom of simply being still.

The Tools That Carried Me

Daily planner, weekly organizer, food journal, budget tracker, Apple Watch, meal prep journal, bullet journals, and clean eating plans. These weren't optional; they were my weapons. Mentally, I had to go all in. I had to put life on pause, deal with sleep deprivation, and be mentally ready to work out 6-7 days a week and hit those daily step minimums. The first week rocked me; the evening classes were no joke. They pushed me, and then, Purpose called me out. First Friday, I was the first one on Zoom, feeling good about myself, and he hit me with it: "Are you showing up 100%?" I was stunned. I thought I was doing well. But I had to be honest, no. I wasn't.

I thought he was about to kick me out. I spent the whole class mentally preparing to get cut. I was upset, but deep down, I knew I needed that push. He told me he had a dream about me holding back. I checked in with my intuitive advisor, and she confirmed it. Purpose was tapped in. He wasn't just leading a challenge; he was leading from vision. The Silent Sundays were life-changing. Silence forced me to sit with myself, to stop distracting, to actually listen. That first Sunday, I was freaking out, thinking I missed a check-in and was about to get eliminated. Turns out, Silent Sundays were optional, and I'm so glad they were part of the process.

By week two, I was begging for my vacation to start. Sleep deprivation was real. Luckily, I had three weeks of vacation lined up. From week three on, I was fully focused, no distractions, locked in. The daily 4:30 AM meditations were a game-changer. I meditated before, but never like this. I dove into Joe Dispenza: "Tuning into New Potentials," and my brain literally started operating on a different frequency. I'd read about Theta states and heart coherence, but during this Challenge, I experienced it firsthand.

After doing it for six weeks straight, meditating daily feels like second nature now, effortless. The level of synergy and coherence I've tapped into since is nothing short of magical. Without my usual YouTube rabbit holes to fall into, I finally had the space to study the science behind Joe Dispenza's work instead of just scrolling. I started listening to "Becoming Supernatural" and "Breaking the Habit of Being Yourself", and for the first time ever, I truly understood and experienced the benefits of deep meditation. During the Challenge, I bought the Joe Dispenza Pineal Gland meditation, and wow, those experiences were otherworldly. That alone was worth the journey. But what made the Unbreakable Woman Challenge so powerful for me was this: it gave me the structure and space to commit to the things I already knew I needed, daily meditation, journaling, and moving my body, but had always put off. It forced me to show up consistently and create the habits I'd only ever dabbled in.

I had never, ever committed to clean eating, let alone documenting every bite with full accountability. I was the type who spent all day grinding for my job and business, constantly grabbing food on the go. Cooking? Meal prepping? That was a luxury I told myself I didn't have time for. But the Challenge didn't give me the option to stay in that cycle, and I'm so glad. Thankfully, I already curbed my sugar addiction and had a decent diet, but being forced to meal prep reintroduced me to the joy of cooking. One of our first assignments was to create a cooking video, and I had so much fun that I made a few more, but I never even posted them. Documenting every meal pushed me to create food that was not only healthy but also beautiful.

During the challenge, I started having uncomfortable hot flashes and other perimenopausal symptoms. That motivated me to take food as medicine seriously and find natural ways to help my body reset. I completed my first 72-hour water fast during the Challenge (yes, 72 hours) and read "The Menopause Reset" and "Fast Like a Girl" by Dr. Mindy Pelz. I also adopted intermittent fasting, and I'm not exactly sure which one did it, but my hot flashes stopped. Between that, eating clean, and doing the emotional detox work through Illuminations, I dropped 10 pounds in six weeks.

The journaling changed my life. Writing first thing in the morning every day for six weeks straight turned journaling into a non-negotiable in my daily life. I made it fun, too; my 8x11 bullet journal was decked out in stickers, colorful Sharpies, and gel pens. I created a practice I looked forward to. I documented my Insights, HDIF (How Do I Feel), Gratitude, Wins, Goals, Inspired Actions, "I Am" statements, and Intuitive Nudges. Looking back, I wish I had written even more detail, especially knowing I'd eventually be sharing this story. Watching myself evolve week by week through those pages was heartwarming, affirming, and humbling. Then, there was class.

Let me say this: the soul of the Challenge lies in the instructors, three powerhouse women and one brilliant man, guided by the fearless leadership of our director. They poured everything into us. They put their own lives on hold to help us step into ours. Every week brought at least one workshop that would rip your stuff wide open, hold it up in front of you, and make you deal with it. The breakthroughs came fast and deep.

THE MIRROR EXERCISE

Week two, Kauri's class. Whew! Brutal. Looking yourself in the mirror and telling the truth, raw, unfiltered, in front of a group of women you barely know? It shook me. But it exposed a blind spot I'd been operating from my whole life: I had been dimming my light to fit inside my parents' vision for me. That realization cracked something wide open in me.

THE EULOGY EXERCISE

We had to write our own eulogies. Mine began: "Arletta was a brilliant soul. A spark never fully ignited..." I wrote about the years I spent surviving instead of thriving, and how I shrank myself to stay safe. Writing those words broke something off me. It was like mourning the version of me that never lived her full truth and then making the vow to never let that happen again.

The Faith Gap

I'd be lying if I said everything about the Challenge sat well with me. One thing that occasionally made me feel out of sync was the heavy Christian emphasis. I didn't know going in that Christianity would be so deeply woven into the sessions. I've always had love and respect for Jesus, but I've never been a Christian. I was raised Muslim, and even then, I eventually outgrew the structure of organized religion altogether.

My spiritual path now is more esoteric, fluid, deeply connected to ancient wisdom and the Divine Feminine. So, when comments came up about "those who don't believe in Christ being doomed," it was jarring. Some moments felt deeply un-Christlike in spirit, and I had to sit with that discomfort. I realized this wasn't the space for me to be fully seen or spiritually understood. And that was okay. I wasn't here for validation. I was here to grow. To be challenged. To build discipline.

So, I made a decision: to stay grounded in my "why," fall in line, and get everything I came for. If you're not Christian and thinking about joining this Challenge, take this into consideration. You'll need to hold your own spiritual integrity while navigating a space that leans heavily Christian.

Final Thoughts

The Unbreakable Woman Challenge was more than I could have ever imagined. It over-delivered on every promise. I'm still in awe of the time, energy, love, and fierce commitment that Purpose, Tameika, and our instructors, Bridgette, Rhonda, and Kauri, poured into us. This Challenge wasn't just a program. It was a rebirth. I've invested thousands in coaching programs, masterclasses, and personal development. But nothing has come close to the transformation I experienced here. And this Challenge? It's free. All it costs is your time, sweat, focus, and commitment.

Honestly, this program is worth $20K–$30K easy. But it's not just the price, it's the value—six intense weeks of coaching, accountability, sisterhood, vulnerability, growth, sweat, and spirit. I came out more focused, more disciplined, more confident, and most importantly, more whole. And to the sisterhood that was born through this experience? You are phenomenal. I've never walked through a transformation with women as honest, courageous, and committed to rising as these.

I now know without a doubt: the pieces of myself that were revealed and healed through this Challenge. They made me Unbreakable, and graduating from this program? One of the proudest moments of my life.

Ebony Brinson

Severed for a Purpose

It's hard to point to just one thing because, truthfully, it was everything. I was stuck in my head, emotions, and life. I had become my own biggest obstacle. Everywhere I turned, I saw people who didn't pour into me, only pulled from me. Takers surrounded me, those who saw my heart, time, and effort as something to consume. Sadly, I let them. I let them drain me until I ran on fumes, leaving me with nothing left.

I wore my pain like a badge on my sleeve; open, visible, and raw, which made me easy prey. People could see I was vulnerable. They could sense I wanted love, acceptance, and peace. They used that against me, manipulating me and taking advantage of my weaknesses. I didn't know how to say no. I didn't have the strength or the belief that my voice ever mattered.

I was silent when I should've spoken, still when I should've moved, agreeable when I should've resisted. The worst part was that I believed I deserved the emptiness I was living in. Then I remembered something. That good ole phrase, "If you want something done right, you must do it yourself." So, I did. I said yes to change. That's when Dr. Tameika Marrow introduced me to the Unbreakable Woman Challenge. She told me, "Straight up, this isn't all fun and games." I laughed a little, thinking, "Good! I like a challenge." Little did I know, this wasn't the kind of challenge you compete in against others; it was the challenge where you face yourself.

This was the kind of challenge that strips you to your core and dares you to rebuild yourself without apology, without fear, and without the old you holding you back. I didn't know it then, but I was about to go through the fire. The first week hit like a brick wall. I was already waking up before 4:30 a.m., reading scripture, and praying. Now, I had to show my progress, document it, and be seen. "Oh Lord! I hate to be seen." That was new. I hated being watched, especially online. Social media never felt like a safe space. But here I was, accountable, transparent, and exposed.

The first real punch came with the mirror challenge: Instructor (Rhonda Sue), "The mirror never lies." That's what I said to myself while staring back at what I saw to be a hideous reflection of myself. I saw a woman I didn't recognize. A woman who had been abused mentally and emotionally, not just by others, but by herself. I had become the echo of every rejection, every betrayal, every lie I had ever been told. I saw the weight of my trauma in my own eyes, childhood wounds, toxic relationships, and mistakes I had never forgiven myself for. "How did I let this happen? How did I get here?"

The answer hit harder than the first day of class. My inner voice told me how I ended up in class, "because you never said no, because you never believed you were enough, and because you gave your body to someone who never wanted your heart. You called that love." That realization crushed me, but the journey didn't stop there. Week by week, I was torn down and rebuilt. I learned to say no in a dozen ways; I learned a new tune to sing using the word "No." It has a ring to it if you embrace it, "LOL."

I knew that putting others first only works when you're not putting yourself last. I realized I couldn't help anyone else until I helped myself. I couldn't heal what I refused to feel. Most of all, I had to forgive myself, not just them, but me. Forgiving myself marked the beginning of a new chapter. To love myself was the transformation. Setting boundaries? That was my salvation. Because healing isn't just a process, it's a fight. I finally stopped fighting myself.

I'll never forget the tough love I received, especially from instructors Kauri Mowell and Joseph Gause. It was raw, liberating, and the kind of truth I had never heard from a man before. After every class, I'd sit alone and let their words marinate. Sometimes, I even cried, upset with myself for what I had allowed to happen to me. "Damn, how did I become so naïve and STUPID?" Some of those words still echo in my soul to this day. Joe would ask, "Are you a lion or a water buffalo?" Kauri would say, "How are you going to sleep tonight?" Little did they know, at that time, I wasn't sleeping. I was up most nights, trapped in a cycle of overthinking, replaying every moment I poured into others, only to watch them thrive while I remained stuck, tired, and invisible.

I thought about how often I had been the water buffalo, trampled, mauled, and emotionally destroyed by the same predators I kept feeding. It wasn't just emotional anymore; it became physical. The stress, the anxiety, the bitterness? It was making me sick. Then I realized something: I wasn't stuck; I was in the wilderness. God had placed me in a spiritual detox, two years of stripping away old survival tactics, outdated mindsets, and generational dysfunction. Because where He was taking me, the old version of me couldn't go.

In that wilderness, I learned something powerful: I am being molded and prepared. God is shaping me with every trial, every tear, every quiet moment of surrender. Each day I seek His face, my mind is renewed. My goals are now aligned with His Word. My path is now lit with His direction. There was one more lesson, one of the hardest of all. I had to let go of the man I had lived with for 13 years. Unmarried, unmatched, unequally yoked.

What Made Me Unbreakable

I can confidently and proudly say that I am now an Unbreakable Woman. But what does that mean? I sat for a long time, reflecting on the journey that had brought me here. Life has had its ups, downs, and a fair share of challenges thrown my way. Before taking this course, I didn't realize that life was living me; I wasn't truly living my life. I was merely doing the bare minimum, stuck in a cycle of responsibility, but never stepping into my dreams. I let fear of rejection keep me from opportunities, allowing others to manipulate and use me, and climb to the top while standing on my back. I silenced my voice, failing to set boundaries, constantly pleasing others to the point that I forgot how to please myself. I procrastinated, convinced that what I had to offer wasn't enough. I was my own worst critic.

During these six weeks, I developed self-awareness, learned about the power of setting boundaries, recognized the reality of manipulation tactics, understood the paradox of people-pleasing, and came to appreciate the importance of holding myself accountable for my choices. I was lacking discernment. But rather than drown in regret, I chose to rebuild. One of my most impactful exercises was writing my eulogy, imagining myself completely gone. Not just my old self, but me leaving my children behind without fulfilling my purpose, without making my mark on the world, without building a legacy. That thought shook me. It made me realize that my work isn't done.

Growth doesn't stop until we take our last breath. We should never stop learning, reading, and connecting with others because you never know what wisdom you might gain from a single conversation. Keep pushing, grow, and, most importantly, stop dimming your light to make others comfortable.

What It Means to be Unbreakable

To me, being unbreakable means facing your fears head-on, refusing to run from discomfort, and instead, strategically breaking down and rebuilding every broken piece. It requires discipline, structure, and execution. It means walking in your purpose, knowing who you are within yourself, and anchoring that identity in the one I call Jesus Christ, the Healer and Redeemer of the world. My entire life shifted once I stopped putting everything before God and myself. Doors that once seemed locked began to open. I learned to prioritize my time to focus on what truly matters. "I know what I want, and I am going to get it!" The Toughest Week: Breaking Old Habits. Week 1 was the hardest.

I remember thinking, "What the hell did I sign up for?" I didn't want to be monitored, but then I shifted my perspective: "If I'm serious about myself, then I want others to see that I'm serious too." What was challenging was fighting my thoughts and staying consistent. In those quiet moments of solitude, doubt consumed me. (You're an author? Your writing is trash. Who's going to heal from your garbage? Who cares? Who's going to listen? That man you wasted 13 years of your life with, yeah, he NEVER LOVED YOU! He left you alone with two kids to raise by yourself. You pushed him away! What will you do about it? He never cared about you or the kids. All he wanted was your body and a warm place to stay! You are a depressed, worthless nothing. You're ugly, that's why you're alone, you're too skinny, you have absolutely nothing to offer!" Those voices in my head would cripple me and drag me into the deepest, darkest, and unsafe places I've ever been.

Day after day, my voice tried to break me. I broke down crying, believing the lies, until I realized that every single one of them was a deception meant to keep me stagnant. The enemy was trying to trap me in a cycle of doubt, fear, procrastination, and depression. He wanted to distract me and keep me far away from God. But I turned to God's Word. Now, I no longer hold on to the patterns of this world. I was transformed by the renewing of my mind through God's word. I read, prayed every morning, and built my relationship with my Savior. The more I did, the more I realized who I was, not broken, not worthless, but unbreakable.

Facing Myself

I'll never forget another complex challenge. "They were all hard!" It might sound simple to some, maybe even silly, but for me, it was deeply personal: taking myself out on a date. Just me, alone at a restaurant, exposed under the weight of prying eyes. The thought of it made me anxious, and nervous tears welled up before I even left the house. It wasn't just about being alone in public. It was about being seen. Really seen.

I felt violated before I even got dressed, imagining strangers staring, judging eyes. Men looking at me made my skin crawl. Women silently measured me up because I didn't fit the "standard." I didn't have a BBL or fake lip fillers. I didn't want any of that; I just wanted to be accepted and seen for myself. I felt like I wasn't enough. Not by society's standards, and that rejection pierced deeper than I could explain.

I broke down and reached out to Rhonda; I couldn't hold it together anymore. It was so bad that Rhonda had to call reinforcements. That's when our leader, Tameika, FaceTimed me. As I watched the phone ring, I thought of not answering it. When I did, I tried to hide the tears, but she saw straight through me. I'll never forget what she said: "The enemy is trying to distract you because you're on your purpose, not on my watch, kid!"

Back then, I didn't fully understand. But now? I get it. The enemy will use anything to pull you away from your calling. To rob you of your identity. To make you forget the truth of what God has already said about you. That I am fearfully and wonderfully made. That I am created in His image. That I am called for such a time as this. In that moment, I repented. I asked God to forgive me for being so cruel to myself, for believing the lies over His truth.

The next day, I got up and put on the outfit I had bought but never felt worthy enough to wear. I zipped up my boots, lifted my chin, and took myself out. I walked into that restaurant alone, and for the first time in a long time, I enjoyed my own company. Yes, at first, it felt awkward. Sitting there, watching couples laughing, families smiling, and children clinging to their parents. My own family? Torn apart. My heart ached. But then I took a deep breath and thanked God. Not just for that moment but for the other families I saw joined together too; that's when everything shifted, and my perspective changed.

I realized that happiness can be fleeting. But peace, true peace, is a posture. A state of being that only God can craft within you. It must be taught, shaped, and refined in solitude and surrendered in faith. From that day forward, I handled life differently. I stopped reacting and started responding with peace. I began to discern who was truly for me and who wasn't.

I stopped chasing approval, and I stopped trying to fit in. The truth is, I was never meant to fit in. I was made to stand apart and stand out. I am a peculiar being, set apart for a purpose greater than me. I finally understand not everyone is meant for me, but that won't stop many from trying to dim my light. But here's the thing, my light? It was never theirs to have.

Water Buffalo or Lion?

From day one, Joe singled me out, of all people, to be the time stamp monitor. I froze on camera, thinking, "Wait… why me? Do I really stand out that much? Dang it." I couldn't say no. That role meant I had to interrupt Joe's class to let him know when he was running overtime or approaching the close. Sounds simple, right? But for me? It felt like a setup! Why? Because I was intimidated by Joe, He reminded me of a drill sergeant. Angry but honest to the point where it hurt my feelings, and that's what I needed.

His voice didn't just speak; it roared like a fierce lion. As for me? I felt like the poor water buffalo just trying to survive in his class! Joseph Gause asked us: "Are you a water buffalo or a lion?" The analogy was clear. Water buffaloes are prey, too friendly and trusting, talking too much without asking the right questions, or worse, not talking enough, not listening, or comprehending information. Failing to observe and be aware of your environment. A lion, though, moves with wisdom, precision, and strength. They are aware, disciplined, and unshakable. They strike with accuracy and precision. That is what I've learned through the Unbreakable Woman Challenge. This journey has redefined me. I no longer live in fear, doubt, or regret. I walk boldly in my purpose, with confidence, knowing God has already equipped me for everything He has called me to do.

Discipline Over Motivation: The Key to Transformation

During my six-week challenge, I gained a significant amount of knowledge that helped transform my life. I want to give a huge shoutout to the incredible instructors who pushed me beyond my limits, helping me develop self-awareness and personal growth skills. They helped me realize I am enough in my own eyes. I am doing well, and I still have room for improvement. I've opened my eyes to my reality and what it takes to rise above it.

Here's the truth: "Motivation might spark action, but discipline sustains it." We don't need motivation; we need discipline. Discipline is a mindset, a commitment to a structured, strategic routine of consistency, and the willpower to stick to it. Motivation is the push to step outside our comfort zones and speak up in those uncomfortable situations. But what happens when you don't feel motivated? There are countless ways to fuel our drive. Listen to an uplifting song, exercise, or a word of encouragement from a friend or even a stranger, but motivation must be replenished. Discipline, however, sustains itself.

Discipline keeps us balanced against our ego. The Lord sustains the righteous. Consistency over perfection. Happiness over ego. With discipline, ego has no place. Discipline is about showing up even when you want to quit, even when you don't know the outcome. Even when the road gets tough, you must show up for yourself; being authentic leads to transformation. So, ask yourself: Who am I? What was I put on this earth to do? Through prayer and meditation, the answers will be revealed.

The Power of Accountability

I learned that having an accountability partner is a game-changer. (Ecclesiastes 4:9) states, "Two are better than one because they have a good return for their labor." According to my research, people with accountability partners are more likely to achieve their goals with a sixty-five percent chance! Find someone to share your habits and goals with. Check in weekly to share progress and uplift each other. A little note to self, "Be mindful, never surround yourself with those who resist growth, remain unadaptable, and refuse change." God will sustain us. One of my favorite scriptures is Jeremiah

29:11. It reminds me that God has a plan for my life, and I will see a bright and beautiful future if I hold onto his promises in my heart and mind with hope.

Professor Gause also spoke on the following lesson: "It takes 21 days to form a habit, so how many days have you not shown up for yourself?" It is easy to get comfortable with habits that distract us from our goals. A small habit can grow into a monstrous addiction. Healed people say "NO," and Fixed people say NO to themselves. If you constantly say yes to others at the expense of yourself, seeking validation that will never come, take a step back. How often have you shown up for people who don't value or show up for you? Reflect on that. Some people in our lives are distractions. Those who watch you struggle but never help, those waiting for your downfall. Those who recognize your potential and try to alter your path, and those who keep you distracted from your focus.

Surround yourself with those who uplift, inspire, support, and motivate your purpose and cause. There is a scripture that reminds me not to pull anyone down but to try to advance yourself. If so, it would be better for you to have a millstone tied around your neck and be drowned in the sea. Sounds harsh, but imagine killing someone for your own gain? How would that sit in your heart? We are put on this earth to help each other grow. We plant the seed, and God waters it. Everyone isn't kind at heart, though, so be careful of the company you keep; you will start to acquire bad habits that will hinder your growth and set you in a place of stagnation. Don't let others cause you to stumble, and don't cause yourself to stumble for validation that you'll never get.

From Habits to Lifestyle

Instructor Joseph taught me that it takes 90 days to turn a habit into a lifestyle. Small, consistent actions create massive change. Setbacks will happen, and they are part of the journey after meditating on the word of God. I realized how many times Jesus forgave those who betrayed him. Even during the crucifixion, being beaten, stoned, and violated, Jesus still asked God, "Forgive them, for they sin and know not what they do." My point is to forgive them, forgive yourself, and start again quickly. Scripture reminds me that God will remove my sin as far as the East is from the West. Every restart strengthens you.

Discipline fuels endurance, and endurance reinforces discipline. It all starts with a decision. When you learn to form simple habits, it can start a structured routine, such as journaling, drinking more water, eating healthier, meditating, and reading, which can create long-lasting change. Consistency is key; choose one habit for the next 21 days and track your progress. Know who your enemy is: Self-Sabotage.

What have you done to become your own worst enemy? The thoughts you entertain and the choices you make either build you or block you. Before this challenge, I had a solid routine, but my mind played tricks. I fell into depression. The things I loved no longer interested me. I dragged my feet on everything. I fed into that mindset, and I manifested more frustration, stress, and stagnation. I let people dictate my emotions and actions. While they lived their best lives, I was stuck in sadness, grieving the loss of my best friend and mourning a 13-year relationship that ended, but when I put myself first. You know what I realized? I realized I was used all along. My mentor instructed me, "Don't be angry if you helped someone grow while they broke you down." My head was hot; I felt steam blowing out of my ears, nose, and head. I was infuriated! How can you tell me, "DON'T GET ANGRY."

Heal and move on. It's easy to dwell on the pain, but it's better to focus on how to move forward. Silence your mind, take a walk, read, embrace nature, and redirect your focus. There's a bigger picture. I asked myself, "What have I allowed myself to do?" Self-overthought to the point of paralysis, self-allowed procrastination to take over, and self lets emotions control actions. How did I overcome it? Discipline. Self-control over emotions, strategic planning, seeking wisdom, and finding a support system. "To know your enemy is to know yourself." What have you created in your mind? What are you truly capable of? You are capable of breaking and rebuilding yourself better than before. Joseph also taught me, "Capital is family, power, decision-making, and discernment." With more meditation in the Word of God, scripture tells us, "The wise woman builds her house, but with her own hands the foolish woman will also tear the house down."

Character & Legacy

Judge people not by their words but by their character and the fruits they bear. By the fruits of their heart, you will recognize who they really are. What do people in your life produce? Do they bring love, joy, and peace? Or do they bring chaos, envy, and division? Discipline, self-awareness, and transformation, your journey starts with a decision. So, let me ask you: are you showing up for yourself?

It Starts at Home

Everything begins with the relationships we build, our connection with our parents, children, and spouses. A strong foundation at home shapes the future, yet many of us grew up without the discipline, guidance, or love needed to show up for others healthily. Too often, people carry an "it's all about me "mentality, not realizing that every action affects the entire household. Saying "yes," we want to say "no," avoiding conflict, and constantly putting others before ourselves are all signs of people-pleasing. But why do we do it? To fight off low self-esteem, we have to dig deep and tell ourselves NO to the things and people who dull our shine, hinder, and stunt our growth." A powerful class taught by Bridgett Whitney taught me that I must let go of the mindset of pleasing others, and I have work to do to please myself.

Set boundaries. Think about the role you've played in strained relationships. Did you stop yourself from speaking up? What strategy did you use to silence your own needs? Triggers and activators often stem from unresolved experiences, childhood trauma, divorce, or past rejection. Emotional responses override logical thinking, resurfacing as triggers of unhealed wounds. One method I was taught that changed my perspective is simple but powerful: Pause, Breathe, Reflect." Another phenomenal lesson taught by Professor Gause is "Pause. Stop before reacting. Breathe. Calm your nervous system. Lastly, Reflect. Choose an intentional response.

Our children need us, but that doesn't mean we neglect ourselves. There's a time for family, and there's a time for self-care. As women, we must learn to put ourselves first, not in selfishness but in strength. Stop prioritizing how a man places you on a pedestal. Learn to set boundaries, stand firm in your purpose, and recognize that your destiny is higher than your desire to please others. A man is called to be on his purpose, just as a woman is called to hers. When both walk in alignment, they fulfill God's design for partnership. A man is supposed to leave his father and mother and be joined by his wife, and the two will become one. United in Christ. Ask questions and expect answers respectfully. Honor yourself by knowing your worth and never losing sight of the purpose God has for you.

God, in His infinite love, has given us something powerful: free will. God won't force Himself into our decisions. He waits patiently, lovingly, for the moment we invite Him in. For years, I was doing what I wanted, living by my own choices, making my plans, and ignoring the quiet whisper of His voice trying to call me higher. While God is merciful, there comes a time when He allows us to feel the weight of our decisions, not to punish us, but to redirect us.

At the start of 2023, I finally got tired of doing life my way. I got on my face, crying and snotty-nosed in prayer. I prayed a dangerous prayer, "God, remove every person who is a hindrance in my life, every distraction pulling me away from Your plan and purpose for my life." I didn't expect what came next. People I thought were permanent started disappearing. Relationships I thought I couldn't live without fell apart. Connections I once depended on were suddenly severed. Just like that, they dropped like flies. It wasn't pretty. It wasn't painless, but it was purposeful. It's what needed to happen.

See, when you ask God to cleanse your circle, He will. But don't expect Him to clean gently. Sometimes, He removes what we cling to the most, not to harm us but to heal us. I had to learn that not every exit is an attack, and not every separation is spiritual warfare. Some things are lessons; scripture reminded me, "In all things, God works for the good of those who love him, who have been called according to his purpose." After He delivered me from over five years of opioid and fentanyl abuse, I learned to recognize His voice: clear, firm, and familiar.

God didn't just speak in my victories; He spoke in my valleys. I've come to realize, "The enemy doesn't design some things. They're designed by God to teach us forgiveness and humility." It wasn't the devil this time. It was discipline, it was love, and it was grace in disguise. God had to empty my hands so He could fill them with better. He had to humble me so He could lift me. He had to teach me that sometimes, the enemy we're fighting is our own will, and the only way to win is to surrender. I've learned that when you finally stop chasing what's not from God, you make room for what is. There is no turning back when God calls you. When He calls you, it's hard to resist His call.

Before the challenge, I've allowed myself to stay stuck in my betrayal of myself and a man who betrayed me, too. He showed little interest in my goals, purpose, or growth. But I held on anyway because I wanted it to work; I needed it to work. Then God spoke, not with thunder or lightning, but with clarity; "The Book of Hosea." I cried after reading it! It hurt; it crushed me to realize I had been trying to build a future with someone I was never meant to build with. I was focused on him, not on Him. I was chasing human validation when Christ had already validated me.

I was waiting for a man to love me, not realizing I was already chosen, accepted, and unconditionally loved by the King of Kings. Letting him go didn't close a door. It opened PLENTY! Because when God calls you to do a thing, there is no going back. When He delivers you from a thing, don't return to it. I'm not the same woman I was. I'm no longer the prey. I'm no longer waiting for approval. I am walking in my purpose. I am standing in truth, and now? I sleep peacefully like a lion in the shade of the trees.

Called For More

We are called to be self-sustaining, but true sustainability is impossible without Christ. Pain can break or shape you; let it teach discipline and consistency. Don't waste your pain on people or situations that don't matter. Instead, use it as fuel to rewrite your history. I once became an addict through pain and loss, and was consumed by it. But pain alone won't sustain you; it can't be your motivation to stay where you are. Pain is meant to push you toward transformation, not stagnation. Darkness, though painful, is what prepares you for the light. It's in the darkness, covered and planted in our dirt of disappointment, guilt, and hurt. That's when the renewal begins. Darkness and isolation are a phase of growth, a season of walking through the wilderness of discovery, and ultimately, a journey toward acceptance in yourself and Christ. Let the darkness refine you, not define you. The light is coming, and it's worth the wait. Thank you, Instructor Kauri, for that amazing lesson. When you focus in class, you are able to express all the information you've retained to save lives.

I Shine Whole Through the Mirror of Brokenness

All in all, the Unbreakable Woman Challenge didn't just challenge me; it changed me. I walked in one way, and I walked out transformed. Along the way, I gained something I never expected: an unbreakable sisterhood. Women who, like me, carried pain, doubt, and stories of hurt but showed up anyway. To witness us rise together, unapologetically and beautifully, reminded me that we were never meant to walk this road alone.

I was blessed with not just one accountability partner but a few. I grew close to three incredible women, sisters I can call, check on, pray with, and who do the same for me. That kind of connection is priceless. I'll be honest: when it came time to "divorce myself," I was angry. After class, I wrestled with what I heard. My verdict? It hit home. It was partially true, and that truth stung. The sting was necessary; I had to face what I had been denying. I was guilty of procrastination and of clinging to my comfort zone. Afraid to let go because loneliness had become familiar.

When graduation day came, everything shifted. "OH YEAH, it's about to go DOWN!" That moment? That was activation. Not long after, the doors opened. Deals, proposals, and opportunities I had prayed for started to find me. The chains were broken. It wasn't because of luck; it was because I stopped focusing on everyone and everything else and started honoring myself and putting God first. It's also about the divine connection of God. I started celebrating my wins, big and small; I told myself, "Every little bit counts," "Keep pushing; you got this." "You're almost there". "It's hard, but don't give up! This is far beyond you, and you can't let God down!" That was my motivation, and guess what? It worked! I dragged myself out of the darkest place, trusting God and leaning on my unbreakable sisters.

Tameika, our leader, has become a living testament to power and resilience. Through every word she spoke, I saw strength forged in betrayal, in heartbreak, in healing. She taught me that pain doesn't have to break you; it can shape you if you give it to God. If you focus. Suppose you prepare for the promise. God's promise. Today, I'm walking boldly in my purpose. Do I still feel fear? Absolutely. But I fight it with the truth; "For God has not given me a spirit of fear but of POWER, LOVE, and a SOUND MIND." A disciplined mind, a sober mind, and a renewed mind.

To whoever is reading this, walk in your purpose unapologetically. No filter, raw and uncut. Feel the pain, but don't stop there. Grow from it. Don't stay stagnant for too long. You never know who's watching. You never know who's waiting for you to rise so they can believe it's possible for them to.

Shannon D. Perkins

The Woman I Had to Lose to Find Myself

Before I entered the Unbreakable Woman 6-Week Challenge, I would have told you my life was going pretty well. Work was work, some days better than others, but manageable. I had a circle of family and friends I loved deeply, and we enjoyed laughter-filled moments, get-togethers, and the kind of late-night conversations that reminded me I wasn't alone in this world. I had met someone new, someone who intrigued me and made me feel seen, and for once, the feelings seemed to be mutual. I was traveling, exploring new places and spaces, and I had finally committed to taking care of my body again. I was eating better, hitting the gym three times a week, and slowly seeing glimpses of the woman I wanted to become again staring back at me in the mirror.

Don't get me wrong, life still had its ups and downs. But if you asked me back then, I would've said, "I'm doing alright. I'm holding it together." At least, that's what I told myself. In all this *life-ing*, I watched my best friend navigate her chaotic chapters, juggling motherhood, building her career, running businesses, nurturing relationships, and still showing up for everyone around her with strength and grace. From the outside looking in, I thought, "She's doing it. She's handling it.

She's winning." Little did I know, she was waging silent battles that no one could see, spiritual warfare, emotional strain, and resistance from people and forces trying to block the purpose, peace, and promise God had over her life.

She told me about someone, a man named Joseph Gause, better known as Purpose and Resilience. She had come across his TikTok and YouTube videos, which were short yet powerful messages that spoke directly to the soul. She said, "Sis, there's something about him. The way he breaks things down, it's real, it's raw, and it's healing." He had created something called Self-Empowerment University and was launching a four-week course focused on emotional healing, personal accountability, mental wellness, and purposeful living. She took a leap of faith and signed up.

I watched her transform. With each passing week, something in her shifted. She was lighter, not because life got easier, but because she was getting stronger. She confronted truths, released old wounds, and started walking in her power in ways I had never seen before. By the end of the course, she graduated with a renewed spirit, and I was so incredibly proud of her. God wasn't finished. That graduation was only the beginning. Soon after, Joseph and my best friend began collaborating. Their shared vision and fire gave birth to something powerful, a new course, specifically for women. It was a sacred space. It was a call to rise. With that, "Unbreakable Woman" was born.

When the Shine Fades and the Spirit Cracks

I wasn't sure if I was truly ready for this. When the Unbreakable Woman 6-Week Challenge was first presented to me, I hesitated. I found myself sitting with it, quietly, anxiously, weighing the decision over and over again. It wasn't that I didn't want to grow or heal. I just wasn't sure if I had the strength to face what I might find once I started peeling back the layers. I thought I was doing fine. Maybe not thriving, but managing. I had what I believed was a "great life." Slowly, quietly, everything began to shift.

It started at work. At first, it was subtle; I've always been the dependable one, the helper, the problem solver, the giver. I took pride in showing up for others. At some point, without realizing it, I stopped showing up for myself. I was pouring into everyone else's needs, while my own cup was drying up. I fell behind on projects. I lost motivation. Then the self-doubt crept in, that quiet voice that makes you question your worth, your capabilities, and whether anything you do is really enough.

I started to resent my job, the people, and the energy. The very space I once walked into with confidence had now become the source of emotional drain. My light, once so vibrant and noticeable, started to dim. Even my colleagues noticed; I wasn't the same. My actions, my attitude, and my energy all began to change. The truth is, I didn't even recognize myself anymore.

Somewhere along the way, I had become a people pleaser, bending, stretching, and sacrificing parts of myself to meet the expectations, requirements, and needs of everyone else. I said "yes" when I really meant "no." I made myself available even when I was depleted, and the most heartbreaking part was that I had nothing left to give; many of those same people started pulling away. I kept asking myself, "Why?" "What did I do wrong?" "Wasn't I good enough?" The more I sat with those questions, the more I realized they weren't about them at all. They were a mirror reflecting the truth: I had attached my value to how useful I was to others. Once people got what they needed from me, I was no longer essential in their lives. That truth stung, and it cracked something inside me.

I became emotional. Every day felt heavy, and I was seeking something, anything, to give me clarity, peace, and direction. I didn't want to spiral, but I could feel myself losing grip. I was tired. Not just tired in my body but weary in my soul. Tired of being in my own way, tired of trying to hold everything together when I was silently falling apart. Tired of being strong for everyone else, while neglecting the parts of me that were screaming to be seen and healed.

I knew something had to change. Not next month, not when things slowed down, but now! I needed strength, not just physical but emotional, mental, and spiritual. I needed to finally show up for myself. I needed to go inward, to do the hard work of uncovering wounds, unlearning patterns, and sitting with the silent pain I had buried beneath years of survival. So, after long reflection, I took a leap of faith.

I joined the Unbreakable Woman 6-Week Challenge. My heart was still filled with questions: "What will this require of me?" "Can I handle it?" "What if I fail?" But deeper than all that noise was a whisper from within, one I hadn't heard in a long time, saying, "You are ready. You were made for this." This course wasn't just another opportunity; it was divine intervention, a lifeline, and a sacred invitation to come back home to myself. So, I said yes, not because I was certain, but because I was done living uncertain about who I was becoming.

With that, I made a promise to myself: I will give this my all, I will not hold back, I will prove to myself that I can do hard things and still rise from them stronger. This wasn't just the beginning of a challenge. This was the beginning of my becoming.

From Frustration to Fierce Resolve

When I stepped into the Unbreakable Woman Challenge, I braced myself for growth, but week one hit me like a freight train. I was pissed, overwhelmed, frustrated, and ready to quit. Twice, I was told I risked elimination for missing requirements. That sting of disappointment seared through me, leaving me disheartened and angry. Yet, in the heat of that moment, something in me flipped. I dropped to my knees, tears streaming, and cried out to God, "Lord, I need strength. I need peace. I need resilience and endurance, not just to finish this challenge, but to transform my life!"

I begged Him to carry me, to help me heal, to teach me how to fight, because I refused to let this defeat me like so many things in my past had. God heard my prayers, and he showed up. After that prayer, a calm clarity settled over me. I wasn't merely tackling a six-week program; I was reclaiming my voice, recovering my power, and rediscovering my identity. Even the cooking assignment, one I'd expected to dread, sparked joy. I experimented with clean ingredients, let creativity guide my hands, and found myself dancing through the kitchen, in awe of the woman I was becoming.

Suddenly, I wasn't changing just for me. I wanted to become a beacon, a living testimony that healing is possible, that discipline yields freedom, and that no matter how broken you feel, you are never beyond restoration. I'll be honest; I wasn't entirely sure I could do it. Fear whispered doubts every step of the way. But something in my soul recognized that this challenge was exactly what I needed.

As I shed old habits, I also shed old relationships. Friends I once trusted faded away when they saw me stand up for myself. It stung, but it was liberating, the first act of reclaiming the power I unwittingly handed over. Perhaps the most grueling test was the 4:30 a.m. workouts, six days a week. In those predawn hours, my body ached, my mind begged me to quit, and my emotions wavered between pride and despair.

Each morning, I rose anyway, and with each rep, each stretch, each pounding heartbeat, my fear transformed into fuel. Consistency became my ally. Discipline became my superpower. What I once dreaded became my driving force. I proved to myself that I could stand firm when comfort whispered to stay in bed. Shift my mindset from "I can't" to "Watch me," Rise above every limit I once believed defined me, and guess what? I did.

When the challenge ended, I emerged not just fitter or wiser, but reborn. I carried with me a conviction stronger than any obstacle. That true transformation is born from faith, fierce determination, and the courage to let go of what no longer serves you. Now, I walk forward as proof that the fiercest storms can spark our greatest strength, and that, no matter where you are in your journey, your next breakthrough may be one brave "yes" away.

"CHALLENGES"

Throughout this six-week journey, five assignments reached into the deepest parts of me, shaking me to my core. They demanded my rawest truth, pulled back the layers I had long kept hidden, exposed wounds I thought I'd buried, and in doing so, they began to resurrect the power I forgot I possessed.

Kauri's Mirror Challenge: "The Woman in the Mirror: A Sacred Reintroduction"

Every day, I stood in front of the mirror, going through the motions. Brush my teeth, fix my hair, maybe add a little makeup if I felt like it. That was my routine. My ritual. A moment with my reflection, but never truly with myself. I never really paused to ask: "Who is this woman, Shannon Dionne Perkins, beneath the surface?" Beneath the hair, the makeup, the smile, I wore like armor. I never dared to look past the polished exterior, but then came this challenge, this divine disruption. Suddenly, I wasn't just looking at myself, I was being asked to see myself. To look deep. To go past the motions. To stare into the eyes of a woman I had forgotten to love, and let me tell you it hit different.

Because the woman in that mirror wasn't just me, she was all the parts of me I had silenced and buried. She was broken in places I didn't want to touch; she carried wounds from battles I swore I had overcome, and she was tired. But still standing. I had spent so much of my life pouring into others, lifting, encouraging, praying, and showing up, but when it came to me? I whispered. Instead of shouting, I settled instead of soared.

The mirror didn't just reflect my image; it reflected my truth. My pain. My shame. My guilt. My grief. My rage. All of it, wrapped in silence, waiting to be acknowledged. As I stood there, tears streaming, voice trembling, trying to speak life into the woman I had ignored, something shifted. That moment was sacred. It wasn't weakness I felt. It was release and permission. Permission to heal, permission to feel, and permission to evolve. I was no longer bound to the version of me that just survived. I was awakening the woman who deserved to thrive.

This challenge didn't just change my mindset; it cracked open my soul. It reminded me that healing doesn't come from hiding your wounds, it comes from honoring them. I started to speak to myself like someone I loved. To look at myself with compassion. To see the woman I once dreamed of becoming, and realize: She's already within me. The reintroduction to myself is ongoing. It takes patience, courage, and grace. Nonetheless, every time I show up for that woman in the mirror, not to fix her, not to critique her, but to see her. I stepped deeper into my truth and embraced my journey because I am not just rising, I am returning. Returning to the woman I was always meant to be, and this time, I'm not looking away.

"What's on Your Plate?" Clearing My Plate: A Lesson in Reclaiming Myself

From the very first session, we were asked to examine what's truly sitting on our plates, not just our daily responsibilities like caring for family, working, going to school, or juggling a packed schedule. This time, the focus went deeper. We were challenged to look at what's weighing us down internally, the mental and emotional battles we silently carry, the things we don't write down or speak out loud but feel in our bones every day.

As I sat with that assignment, pen in hand, I started with the obvious: the visible, tangible demands life throws my way. But then I took a breath and began to dig deeper. That's when it hit me. I had been carrying so much more than tasks; I had been carrying pain, pressure, people, and patterns that no longer served me. I had allowed toxic thoughts, destructive behaviors, and emotional baggage to consume space in my mind and heart for far too long. I had been telling myself, "I'm good. I got this. I can handle it," but I truly believed that if I just pushed through, I could keep pretending everything was fine and eventually "Keep it Moving. But let me tell you, that moment of reflection was like holding a mirror up to my soul.

I had to face myself, and I had to be honest. I literally said, "Damn, Shannon, you really need to get your Sugar. Honey. Iced. Tea together." Because the truth is, pretending was no longer serving me. It was time to clean my plate, for real. As Bridgette said in class, "Do the work, Remove the mess." So, I did. Slowly, intentionally, painfully, I began scraping off everything that no longer fed me. By the second part of the session, my plate looked different, lighter, and freer. The negativity I had carried like a badge of endurance was now gone. The weight of other people's expectations was gone; I started separating myself from people, patterns, and even pieces of myself that no longer aligned with the woman I'm becoming.

In their place, I started speaking life back into myself. Hope, healing, power, and peace. This process taught me that clearing your plate isn't just about letting go; it's about making space for who you truly are. It's about owning your healing and reclaiming your identity, your peace, and your purpose. I'm not just checking things off anymore. I'm living lighter. I'm choosing me, and for the first time in a long time, that plate is finally mine again.

Rhonda's Eulogy Assignment/Session

When the assignment was presented, writing my own eulogy, I felt a flutter of nerves. It wasn't a morbid task; however, I never imagined or expected to take on an assignment such as this to speak of myself at my own funeral. "It was weird," sitting in my quiet room, pen trembling in my hand. I felt a weight heavier than mere words. Writing my own eulogy wasn't an exercise in vanity; it was a ritual in courage, one that would demand I unearth both my brightest triumphs and my most painful scars.

I began with my victories. I wrote of successfully graduating from Bowie State University with a Bachelor of Science Degree in the study of Business Management, being a member of Bowie State's choir and recording a live album with gospel star, Richard Smallwood, becoming a mentor providing comfort, support and encouragement to those who suffered heartache, losing someone special and being a person who gave much of myself to others who crossed my path, loving to a fault through not only words but also through actions.

Then came the hardest part, confessing my wounds. Slowing my breath, I confessed to being adopted, not knowing anything about my biological parents, and doing everything within me to attempt to find them or someone I was related to, to no avail. Nothing transpired from my search for any biological family. I confessed to the times when I let toxic friendships dictate my worth, when I whispered, "not enough," instead of shouting, "I belong here." I wrote of grief I'd been carrying for years of my mother's death, my ex-fiancé leaving me, one of my best friends passing from COVID, and me attempting suicide due to my not being able to handle any more trauma, sadness, or death that had already come my way. I named the heartbreak that taught me to build walls, and the shame that nearly convinced me my story wasn't worth telling. The paper blurred with tears, and my hands shook. Exposing these wounds felt like reopening them, but each admission also offered release.

So, as the final sentence settled on the page with the closing of my eulogy just written, I said to myself, "Here lies a woman who refuses to let her wounds write her finale." The shame that once bound me started to lose its grip. The pride I once feared seemed earned. My heart swelled with purpose. I was no longer merely narrating my life; I was actively authoring it.

When it was time for me to present and read my eulogy out loud, virtually, in front of everyone, my voice cracked. The room echoed with my own truths, celebration, and confession intertwined. In that moment, I realized legacy isn't a distant monument built after death; it's the living testimony we compose with every choice and every brave confession made.

This assignment didn't just challenge me to write; it demanded that I become the woman I described.

It reminded me that owning our story, flaws and all, is the greatest act of self-love and empowerment, and with that realization, I felt not just heard, but alive. It also reminded and allowed me to realize that legacy is not a chapter waiting at life's end. It's the pen we hold today, the choices we ink into our story with every breath. Legacy is living. It's the living tribute we compose with each choice, each kindness, and each courageous step forward. Legacy is the tapestry we weave in real time, with the threads of our own truth.

Joseph Gause's "The Empty Cup" Session

When I first logged into Joseph Gause's "The Empty Cup" session, I expected a pep talk, another motivational speech to lift my spirits. Instead, he handed me something far more powerful: a mirror to my own soul. Joseph guided us to imagine our hearts as cups, once teeming with hope, love, and purpose, but now cracked and parched from endless giving. As I closed my eyes, I felt the familiar ache in my chest: the hollow echo of every ounce of care I'd poured into others, never once pausing to refill my own reserves. In that silence, I acknowledged the late nights I wept alone, grieving for the parts of me I'd sacrificed.

With probing questions, Joseph led me to trace a golden thread through my darkest memories, each heartbreak, rejection, and loss woven into the tapestry of my life's purpose. I saw how the grief over my mother's passing, the betrayal of broken friendships, my insecurities of the extra weight I was carrying, and the weight of past failures had become hidden fuel for my resilience. He taught me to bow my head in gratitude, not out of denial, but as an act of radical acceptance: "Thank you," I whispered to my past, "for shaping the strength I carry now, yet with every confession, Joseph showed me how to turn that pain into promise. He taught me to thank my past for its lessons, each heartbreak, each setback, as if they were sacred gifts, not burdens to be banished.

In that virtual room, I discovered that resilience isn't simply "bouncing back." It's the art of bending without breaking, like tall grass that yields to the wind but never loses its roots. I learned that retreating from my own needs had left me brittle, prone to shattering under pressure. Joseph showed me that refilling my cup wasn't a luxury; it was an essential act of stewardship over my body, mind, and spirit. I committed, then and there, to nourishing myself through prayer, honest reflection, and boundaries that protect my peace.

By the end of that session, I realized I had been living on borrowed purpose, lifting others while mine lay neglected. Joseph challenged me to reclaim my "why": the core belief that first set my heart ablaze years ago. As I whispered that purpose back to myself, "to heal, to inspire, to love without reservation." I felt a shift deep within. I left that session with trembling hands and a heart reborn. I vowed to refill my cup daily, not with business, but with intentional practices: whispered prayers at dawn, writing truth until tears flowed, and saying "no" to anything that drained me dry. In embracing my own needs, I discovered my greatest gift, to pour from a cup overflowing with my own worth, so that every drop I give is sourced in the unshakeable knowledge that I, too, am deeply cherished.

The Divorce Decree Letter from "The Old Me"

When the prompt landed, write a divorce decree not for a spouse, but for the old version of myself, my breath caught in my throat. I gathered my courage and a blank page, knowing this would be the most intimate farewell I'd ever pen. I began by honoring the vows I once made to her: the promise to protect her from pain, the pledge to forgive her missteps, the oath to keep her small fears from crowding out her dreams. With each line, I traced the gentle compassion I'd shown that frightened, wounded part of me, acknowledging the loyalty that had carried us through so many storms.

Then, page by page, I named the betrayals she had inflicted upon my growth: the whispered doubts that made me shrink, the excuses that kept me locked in old patterns, the moments I sacrificed my joy on the altar of comfort. Ink spilled like tears as I confronted how she had chained me to regret and shame; how her fear had become my prison. With my heart pounding, I lifted my pen one final time and crossed the page. In bold, unwavering letters, I declared: **"By the authority of my reclaimed spirit, I hereby dissolve this union with the old me. I release the guilt that weighed me down, the self-doubt that silenced my voice, and the comfort of a story that no longer serves my growth. From this moment forward, I choose freedom, courage, and the woman I am becoming."**

As I ceremoniously "served" myself this decree, folding the paper and sealing my intention, I felt the invisible shackles snap. A fierce light flared within me, igniting a torch I would carry into the next chapter of my life. This was more than an ending. It was a baptism of my own making. In that sacred act of separation, I became both the protagonist and the author of my story, no longer haunted by who I once was, but boldly alive in who I am destined to be.

"When the Layers Began to Fall Away"

Each assignment, each moment of reflection, each uncomfortable truth peeled back layers I didn't even realize I was still hiding behind. Layers I had mastered wearing, making me appear strong, composed, and even unshakeable to the outside world, but inside, I was still carrying weight I didn't fully understand, and suddenly, I found myself face-to-face with truths I had spent years outrunning.

Truths I had covered up with business, smoothed over with smiles, and buried so deep that I almost forgot they existed. But here's what I've learned: You never truly know what's festering inside until you are forced to confront it, sit with it, breathe through it, and ultimately deal with it. Not just the polished pieces or with the pain you've "processed" but with the parts of you still bleeding beneath the surface; the stories you tell yourself to cope; the fears you never gave voice to, and the trauma that still whispers in your ear when no one else is around.

This journey stripped me bare. It pulled back the curtains I had carefully closed. It unearthed memories I had sealed shut. It forced me to sit in rooms within myself that I didn't want to revisit. I never anticipated how deeply I would have to wrestle with the unhealed wounds I said were behind me; the pent-up rage I disguised as strength; the toxic thought patterns that echoed, "You're not enough" and the behaviors that once protected me but had since begun to suffocate me, and the hardest part; I thought I knew myself. I really did, but what I came to realize is that I only knew the version of me that had learned how to survive. I didn't yet know the version of me that was capable of healing, growing, or transforming.

There is something terrifying and beautiful about sitting in your own truth. The raw, unfiltered, unedited version. It breaks you open in a way that hurts but also frees. Because when the layers fall away, you no longer have to pretend, you no longer have to perform, and eventually, you are finally able to feel & more than anything, you are finally able to begin again. This part of the journey wasn't about perfection; it was about reclamation. Reclaiming my mind, my peace, and myself. Though it was painful, it was necessary. Because this is how transformation begins: Not with pretending you're whole but with admitting where you're still broken and choosing every day to become whole anyway.

About The Authors

Dr. Tameika A. Marrow is a visionary leader, transformational speaker, and passionate advocate for women's empowerment. As the Director behind *Unbreakable: Rise of the Unshakeable Woman*, Dr. Marrow has dedicated her life to helping women break free from cycles of pain and step boldly into purpose.

With a doctorate in Christian Leadership and Business, Dr. Marrow has years of experience guiding countless women through inner healing and self-discovery. She blends spiritual insight with practical strategies that spark true transformation. Dr. Marrow is also the founder of Unbreakable Woman University, where she equips women to rebuild from the inside out, mind, body, and spirit.

Beyond her work in ministry and personal development, Dr. Marrow runs a thriving consulting business based in Washington, helping leaders and organizations achieve breakthrough success. Most importantly, she is a loving mother to five amazing, bright children who are her daily inspiration and greatest joy. Her mission is simple yet powerful:

to see women healed, whole, and unapologetically walking in their God-given destiny.

Tina Marie is a radiant force, shining with gratitude as she shares her journey with the world. Life hasn't been easy for her; it's been a winding road of challenges, heartbreak, and moments that tested her strength in ways she never imagined. At times, the weight of it all felt unbearable. Trauma and abuse left their scars, but they never defined her. Through resilience, healing, and transformation, Tina discovered the light within herself, and now, she's using her voice to help others find theirs.

Her story isn't just her own; it's a testament to the power of women standing in their truth, unafraid to speak out. Too many carry hidden wounds beneath the weight of fear and shame. Tina's mission is to break that silence, to remind others everywhere that they are not alone, and that their voices matter. Every story has power. Every story deserves to be told.

Eleanor N. Brown is a woman who loves LIFE! She had always known she had a greater purpose in this thing called life when life put her through rape, abuse, depression, heartbreak, and rejection; Nicole STILL smiled, encouraged, and motivated others. Not realizing, she needed HERSELF the most. After being told as a child that she was a mistake, being called a "dumb blonde," she began to feel something rise inside of her. She still did not know what or why, but she knew God had something great in store for her. After a 12-year failed marriage, she began to discover who she was and meant to be, all while being a mother, daughter, baby sister, aunt, cousin, and friend.

December 2, 2024, Nicole decided to take a chance and bet on HERSELF. By trusting a man who was once a stranger, I became a friend, leader, and coach. This man and his team of leaders ushered Nicole into a life of PUTTING ME FIRST, a Sovereign LIFE! My vision of myself is now crystal clear! No GOING BACK, No DOUBT, No STOPPING! I GOT WERK TO DO!!

Raquel Breaux is a dynamic poet and spoken word artist from New Orleans, LA, whose passion for storytelling and self-expression has been a driving force since childhood. With a deep love for words, she weaves poetry that reflects personal growth, hard-earned lessons, and the essence of human experience. Her journey as an artist has taken her to stages across the country, where she has performed solo shows, collaborated with fellow creatives in community productions, and shared her voice in poetry features alongside host Malcolm-Jamal Warner. Whether commanding the mic with raw vulnerability or delivering thought-provoking narratives, Raquel's work resonates with authenticity and heart.

Beyond the stage, Raquel is a force for transformation in her community. As a dedicated life coach, she empowers others to embrace their journeys of healing and self-discovery. She also brings her passion for movement and joy to the dance floor as a ZUMBA instructor. Whether through poetry, coaching, or dance, her mission remains the same—to uplift, inspire, and connect. Now, she embarks on an exciting new chapter, contributing her artistry to this collaborative work. Her words invite readers into a world of reflection, resilience, and revelation.

Lesley Hamilton Burrows was born in Lansing, Michigan. She now resides in North Carolina. She's a proud mother of one incredible and brilliant son, and she spent five years living the military life. Lesley studied Early Childhood Development at the University of Wilmington, NC, but she had a passion for caregiving, where she found joy in helping older people. Through this work, she has learned the power of patience and understanding, two qualities that make life better in every way.

But Lesley isn't stopping there! She's getting her real estate investing license and has big plans to enter the property world, think homes, storage units, hotels, and even billboards! Next year, 2026, Lesley will make another dream come true by traveling the world and embracing new cultures, foods, and experiences. When she's not working or planning her next big move, you'll find her roller skating, baking up something sweet, and just loving life. With her new go-getter attitude and passion for growth, Lesley knows one thing for sure: her future is *bright*!

Jade Otto, born and raised in Phoenix, Arizona, is a driven and creative individual with a passion for continuous learning and self-improvement. She enjoys reading about life enhancement, psychology, nutrition, and astrology blogs, with "The 4-Hour Chef" by Tim Ferriss as one of her favorites. She believes real growth comes from measurable action, pinpointing the goal, jumping in, getting uncomfortable, and adapting when necessary. At 19, Jade dropped out of college and built her first successful Amazon FBA business, proving that determination can lead to success outside traditional paths at any age. She overcame several health challenges through research, trial and error, and tenacity, eventually earning her certification as a nutrition coach. Her knowledge has helped family and friends achieve healthier, happier lifestyles.

In her free time, Jade enjoys long walks, working out, creating makeup looks, and dressing up as fun characters like Lord Farquaad. Currently, she is working toward a career as a professional makeup and hair stylist and developing a clothing line. Jade is now on a path that will give her the freedom to explore new passions, learning to dance, mastering Mandarin, archery, Brazilian Jiu-Jitsu, traveling, and embracing all the experiences life has to offer.

Debra Goodwyn is a loving and dedicated mother of three amazing children and a proud grandmother whose nourishing spirit extends beyond her immediate family. As a devoted caregiver for her mother, Debra symbolizes selflessness and resilience, always putting the needs of others before her own. She is happily retired after a successful career in Information Systems. Debra continues to find purpose in uplifting those around her. Her years of professional experience have instilled in her a strong work ethic and problem-solving mindset.

Debra is naturally optimistic and encouraging. She has a passion for motivating others to reach their fullest potential. Whether speaking words of wisdom, motivation, and encouragement to her family or supporting friends through challenging moments, Debra believes in the power of optimism and perseverance. Even in retirement, she remains actively engaged, embracing each day with gratitude and a heart full of love to share with others in need.

Astride Candice is an educator, aspiring life coach, and digital marketer dedicated to personal growth and empowerment. Originally from South Africa, she now resides in New Jersey, where she cherishes her most treasured role as a mother to her wonderful daughter. With a passion for helping others unlock their full potential, Astride combines her background in education with her drive to inspire and support individuals on their journeys. Her love for travel fuels her curiosity and broadens her perspective, enriching her personal and professional endeavors. Whether through coaching, digital marketing, or everyday interactions, Astride is committed to making a meaningful impact in the lives of those she encounters.

Aderemi Holloway is a writer, creative thinker, and lifelong dreamer passionate about storytelling, transformation, and growth. She graduated from Contra Costa Medical Career College with a certification in phlebotomy and a background in healthcare, but her curiosity extends far beyond a single field. Aderemi loves to travel, explore new cultures, and immerse herself in different ways of thinking, always seeking new perspectives to inspire her journey.

Whether she's diving into her next story or thoughtfully examining life's deeper layers, Aderemi is always searching for meaning and new ways to express it. She believes in the power of yourself, even when it's hard. This book marks the beginning of a new chapter, and she's just getting started.

Arletta Faheemah Saafir came to this planet knowing her purpose and journey through healing, transformation, reinvention, and resurrection as she unearths more authentic versions of her true self. The flesh-embodied soul that is authentic and a walking and talking truth. In her process of divinely guided evolution, she encountered Purpose and Resilience in his YouTube interview on the High-Level Podcast with Princella the Queenmaker. She had been seeking an opportunity to create a more disciplined and focused life, and when she heard Purpose share about the 6-week Unbreakable Woman challenge, she was sold and, in the middle of the podcast, requested to join the Unbreakable Woman group.

In 3D, Arletta is the oldest of 7 children, child-free and single. She was born and raised Muslim and evolved into being spiritually connected and cosmically guided. With degrees in Mathematics and English, Arletta styles herself as a Libra-balanced, right-brained intuitive. Arletta is most passionate about learning, teaching, and drawing the beauty out of every encounter and aspect of life. Professionally, she is the Director of Business Development for an imaging funding company in the personal injury industry. She is also the Creative Director of an Atlanta-based Luxury Event Planning and Wedding Design Studio.

A true polymath and lifelong bookworm, having read thousands of books, Arletta's current obsessions are geopolitics, ancient African history, global economics, and the return and reawakening of the Divine Feminine. In fulfilling her purpose, Arletta is now heeding the call to teach, write, inspire, evolve, and empower. Ultimately, she is expanding her business globally and positioning herself to do business development in the Motherland, bridging the connection to us of African descent in America.

Ebony Brinson is a force, mind, body, and spirit. A proud mother of two brilliant children, she's a self-published, multi-genre author and business owner of Woman of Many Trades, born and raised in the Bronx, New York. Ebony has spent years of her life pouring her soul onto paper for as long as she can remember. Whether it be an eye-catching and vivid graphic design, a soul-filled poem, or a powerful short story, writing isn't just her passion; it's her purpose.

Ebony's creativity doesn't stop there. She's also a singer, having honed her voice at the Boys and Girls Choir of Harlem. Whether through words or music, she's determined to leave her mark on the world, using the gifts God has blessed her with to teach, inspire, and uplift anyone willing to learn. For Ebony, life is about creating purpose, making an impact, and leaving a legacy. She challenges you to think bigger, dream bolder, and fully reach your potential. As she puts it, *"Bright minds create unique futures."* **So the question is, what's on your mind that can shape a bright future for you and those after you?**

Shannon D. Perkins is a motivated, dedicated, and driven professional with nearly two decades of experience in government contracting. She is also a proud graduate of Bowie State University. Her years of dedication, expertise, and commitment to striving for excellence and hard work have made her stand out among many. From a young age, Shannon was drawn to the arts, dreaming of life as an entertainer. She trained in ballet and tap, performed in productions, and sang in school choirs from elementary through college. As a member of the Bowie State University Choir, she had the opportunity to perform alongside the legendary gospel artist Richard Smallwood. Today, music remains a big part of her life; she's often invited to sing at special events, sharing her gift with those around her.

Shannon is on a journey of consistency, transformation, and healing others who have crossed the same path as she has. Prioritizing her health became a mission that led her through a successful surgery that reshaped her outlook on life. With courage and determination, Shannon shares her "Unbreakable Woman" experience to encourage, uplift, and help those who face challenging moments similar to her own. Shannon created a YouTube channel, "LovlySDPerkins." Through personal testimonies, faith-filled reflections, and real-life experiences, her goal is to uplift and empower others to overcome adversity and embrace life's journey with strength and hope.

Everyone has a story, but you don't need to spend your life striving for traditional publishing. Rejection doesn't have to be your path; you don't have to shoulder all the work while publishing companies reap the rewards. There's a thriving community of independent authors, just like you, who are successfully publishing their stories and making a living. Our technological expertise can make the journey to publication a breeze. Let Woman of Many Trades LLC handle the challenging aspects, allowing you to focus on your writing.

Send us your Word Document, and we'll cover the rest. It's that straightforward! Traditional publishing houses often prioritize "celebrity authors" over the everyday writer, making it nearly impossible for first-time authors to break through. However, the landscape has evolved, and self-publishing is now a viable and respectable option. It's no longer considered "vanity publishing." The self-publishing industry empowers authors to get their work published quickly, retain their rights, and earn up to ninety percent of their royalties, a substantial increase from the traditional five to seven percent.

Woman of Many Trades is a versatile and multifaceted business offering a variety of services. Our primary objective is to provide a service that alleviates your needs, whether creating distinctive business logos, crafting compelling written proposals, or assisting with self-publishing. Do you genuinely want to invest all your time in the tedious tasks of formatting, converting, and designing a book cover, not to mention the laborious process of self-promotion? Our team of professional editors is here to relieve you of these burdens. We provide ISBN assignments, enabling you to retain one hundred percent of your rights and facilitate worldwide distribution of your stories through platforms like Amazon and other retailers.

We genuinely hope you'll embark on becoming a published author and part of our expanding Woman of Many Trades family. May you achieve the global recognition you rightfully deserve. You are deserving of success. Remember, success belongs to those who create opportunities, not those who wait for them. Have faith in yourself and believe in your ability to accomplish anything, as it all begins with the power of your mind. Thank you for choosing to join us on your adventure to success!

www.facebook.com/borncreator33

www.instagram.com/woman_ofmany_trades7

www.womanofmanytrades.com

Made in the USA
Columbia, SC
09 September 2025

17f899c8-0178-434b-8a04-3122ee3749c7R01